Praise for Man Alone

From its opening scene on a bar stool, to Zene's denouement, walking into the tunnel of darkness, the novel beguiles the reader with images that arrest, unmask, and reflect Everyman's fated existential dialogue with self. *Man Alone's* stripped-down cadence—peeling away the veneer of words—achieves an apotheosis of carnal sensuality where two bodies combine into one . . . this author's luminous reveal.

—Dennis Must, author of *MacLeish Sq.* et al

Jack Remick has invented a new genre—Pulp Literature. In *Man Alone*, Remick delivers lines with the deadpan of a pulp detective on the crime-trail . . . Remick's characters engaged in the base pursuit of their own ends, burn up in the fire of their own kindling . . . Remick builds on a theory of masks and unmasking, and, in the stunningly poetic images that run in Zene's observations, you see a writer as observer whose characters have depth as well as a fatal blind spot. In *Man Alone* Remick has come into some kind of new literary superpower.

—Christine Runyon, poet

Man Alone is a story that must be experienced . . . the story is wonderfully original, with characters who are exquisite in their flaws . . . Remick's talent with words is unquestionable, and his ability to create such original tales that draw you in and force you to contemplate the realities of the darker side of human nature is, in my opinion, unmatched.

—Theresa Cogdill, artist

Man Alone is . . . rich in character, plot, and language. Remick's characters are twisted, murderous, real—and above all, riveting.

—Jack Smith, author of *Being* and *Run*

Jack Remick's *Man Alone*, the dark story of a defeated man sliding into reckless hopelessness, packs a spare, yet intimate gut punch with unforgettable characters and an impeccable sense of place. Remick is a masterful storyteller. He is that good.

—Eleanor Parker Sapia

Man Alone is Jack Remick at his best. He delivers a cautionary tale of forgotten love and lust wrapped up into a who done it complete with tarnished knight and a fallen princess. Every word and sentence are sharp with the right kind of hurt . . . *Man Alone* draws you in as you wait for the inevitable boy saves girl story. But the outcome will surprise you.

—Tony Ollivier, author of *The Amsterdam Deception* and *The Tokyo Diversion*

In *Man Alone*, Remick's doesn't just tell you a story . . . he makes you experience it . . . observe it, feel the pain, the hurt, the ecstasy, the joy, the sadness of the cast of broken toys, that live in his story . . . This is a book that demands you sit up and pay attention . . . a story that will make you think, will cause others to say, there but for the grace of God, go I. My advice . . . Buy a ticket; you're going to enjoy the ride. I did. 5 Stars!

—Wally Lane, Screenwriting to Industry Standard

Man Alone is classic Jack Remick, a prolific writer who digs deep into the dark underbelly of modern civilization and takes readers to places we don't always want to go. His characters are people we may not want to spend time with but who ask questions we need to address . . . With the skill of a master, Remick keeps us turning pages in a voyeuristic desire to see what happens next like drivers slowing to gawk at high-speed collisions.

—Arleen Williams, author of *The 39th Victim* and *The Alki Trilogy*

Jack Remick explores the lonely, often violent experiences of a straight man in a cold world. *Man Alone* is a brutal look at what some men are willing to do in their search for connection and intimacy.

—Elena Hartwell, novelist,
One Dead Two to Go; Three Strikes You're Dead

Man Alone is dark, funny, vivid, and fast. The people are desperate and they are sexy and they are dangerous. *Man Alone* is about love and beauty and evil. The prose glints and dazzles, page after page. It doesn't let up. It is brilliant. Read this book!

—Priscilla Long, author of *Fire and Stone: Where Do We Come From? What Are We? Where Are We Going?*

Man Alone—a riveting existential story about a man's love for a woman—is a treatise on frustrating passions, dreadful forebodings, disappearance, erasure, death, and silence. It is a compulsion about a man's desire to do "anything to keep from hitting bottom alone." Jack Remick pieces together a world, scene by scene, of broken souls and urban misfits longing to break free from their oppressors . . . In this twenty-first-century tale, Remick, a brilliant storyteller, embeds the good/evil of civilization as a theology of dread that "explained the state of the human in the universe." We are left to ponder "a dead man killing another dead man" and the classical Greek word: *tetelestai*, meaning "It is complete." The Man Alone—"the complete and utter finality of existence"—the silence.

—Geri Gale, novelist, *In The Closet*

With *Man Alone*, Remick has created a striking study of primal man in the throes of desperation and loneliness. Every character is gravely flawed, yet manically interesting…Throughout the entire novel, Remick repeatedly recalls us to the nature of man as an animal whose existence is threatened when rejected, who fights, possesses, and dies for a mate as a matter of existential principle. His use of smell as the leading sense potently grounds us in the primitive mind. This is further emphasized by the animalistic nature of the sexual encounters, the stark and fearless language, stripped format and structure, and wild unanswered questions. Remick has gone rogue in this masterful tale of unanswered yearning. He has created a beautifully disturbing power struggle between man and woman that sears the memory.

—Nicole Disney, award-winning novelist,
Dissonance in A Minor. Hers to Protect. The Clinch.

Man Alone

Man Alone
The Dark Book

Jack Remick

Sidekick Press
Bellingham, Washington

Published 2023
Printed in the United States of America
ISBN: 978-1-958808-15-3
LCCN: 2023911518

Sidekick Press
2950 Newmarket Street, Suite 101-329
Bellingham, Washington 98226
sidekickpress.com

Man Alone: The Dark Book

Cover art by Russ Spitkovsky
Cover design by Andrea Gabriel

*"Carruthers suggests one does not first entertain a
private thought and then write it down:
rather, the thinking is the writing."*

—Andy Clark, *Being There*

Man Alone

The band wasn't any good, but it was loud. Music he didn't care about from musicians he didn't care about rattled around in Zene Morley's head until he couldn't think—and that was good.

He wasn't in the bar to think. He sat on a barstool, shallow breathing with his brain. An electroencephalogram would have shown that, except for the energy it took to heft the stein, he was at the reptilian level. He should have registered with City Light as an energy-saving device. If he ever figured out a way to market himself, he could be rich. But he wasn't rich.

Zene didn't take up much space or consume a lot of resources. He liked it that way. Except for the beer. With the beer, the more he drank, the better he felt.

He sat on the barstool like he had been born and raised there. When other kids were riding tricycles, Zene was practicing his dismount on the kitchen stool. At seven he was an expert at it.

For six hours, he had been drinking. One beer after another at a pace that wasn't wearing the bartender's arm out but wouldn't allow her to run off to the Bahamas between schooners. The last words he had uttered were "Red Hook," five hours and fifty-five minutes before. And now, unless the laws of physics no longer applied, he was going to fall off the stool.

He leaned, the Leaning Tower of Morley, his center of gravity shifting. He'd flop onto the floor and disappear in the sea of peanut shells.

Last one, Zene.

Patty was a large, coarse, and strong woman who had seen drunks in all sizes and shapes, and there wasn't one of them who scared her. She didn't think she had seen everything. She did not believe that Jesus was coming. She did not believe that the earth was flat.

Men came into the bar and amazed her with their stupidity and with the filth they spoke when they thought they were an inch away from going down on her. She didn't go to church on Sunday, and she didn't feel guilty about it—a woman had to earn a living.

With two fingers, she lifted Zene's empty glass. She didn't re-fill it. She wiped the bar with four emphatic swipes of a bar cloth that had soaked up more than a few suds, and which, in her hands, became a weapon. She was a realist who knew when a drunk was running on fumes and wasn't afraid to say so. If they didn't like her voice, she let the towel talk to their eyes. If they still didn't see the point, she grabbed them by the scruff and tossed them out.

Zene didn't give her any grief.

He studied the jet-black hair piled up on her head, surveyed the lines at the corners of her eyes. The mask shielded her mouth, hid her lips. Masks did that.

She was not beautiful, nor was she unattractive, two very different propositions. Zene would have taken one of two things—another beer or a roll in the hay with her. In his suds-soaked state, he understood the glint of cruelty in her eyes, and he knew the chances of getting either were absolute zero. Her eyes broke men's hearts every day.

He scooped up his change and stepped out into the night. He heard her say,

If ever a man was tanked . . .

He took the hard way home, lining up with the curb and hoping he didn't hit any trees. If he did, he didn't care. He didn't care about anything. Nothing. There was caring and there was noth-ingness, and right then he tended toward nihilism. It was a socially irresponsible position, but it was less complicated than carrying the burden of secular involvement. He tried to remember the last time he got involved, but it took a lot of effort that otherwise could have been expended in walking straight, so he gave it up.

He plowed along Northgate Way to the light, then turned up Eighth Avenue. He lost his footing in the dark and skidded in the gravel beside the road. He hit the deck, the gravel grinding the palms of his hands. He folded his arms over his nose. It was good at that time of night—no school kids to make fun of him, no cops to help him home by way of the precinct station. As he lay in the rocks, he lost his hands again. He took a deep breath. No hands. It had happened before. As he lay dying, he had lost his hands under the blanket. He searched with hands now pitted with gravel and he found them again but he didn't understand how that worked. He knew that he was feeling his hands with his hands, but how could that work? Life was not a dream. Life was an hallucination—his hands searching for his lost hands—one of the tricks of the mind in a sick body. The virus was in his brain and his hands had become detached from his body and he knew, without understanding, that he was feeling his hands with his hands, but how could that be?

He got to his knees. Lost in the slosh of beer and the ocean of virus eating his brain, he squared his shoulders, humped his back, and did the hardest thing he'd done in two years—he got to his feet and walked.

Eighth Avenue rises up a hill that's a couple hundred feet from Northgate Way. It crests at 89th. At that point, it is the highest hill in Seattle. If you are sober, it cuts the heart out of you, drunk, you walk it wondering how god could have done that to you and left it in the city.

At 89th, Zene knew it was a mistake to walk home because the exercise was clearing his head. That was one of the dangers of physical activity—it burned off the alcohol instead of letting it turn the anguish of being sober to the peace of nothingness. He fought his way through the approaching fit of sobriety, shivering with fear at the thought of being clear-headed. He turned up the walkway to his place.

It was an older house on Roosevelt Way, the only rooming house left in the Maple Leaf district of Seattle. Everything around it was condos and apartments, ultra-modern boxes, some of them with solar arrays, most without, evidence that most Americans didn't think climate change was the real deal or didn't care about the Greenland ice sheet melting. In the lemming culture, people became part of a huge machine, all going lockstep in the same direction, chanting hosannas to owning things before running off the cliff of debt.

The house couldn't last much longer. A big place like that on prime real estate would get some hotshot's eye and a few hundred thousand bucks later, it would become the future.

But first they had to get past Dora Miller. Zene's landlady. She was the last outcropping of the eroded American spine, a relic of another time when people stood up straight, weren't afraid of the truth, and had respect for one another. At eighty-three, she drove her own Buick, cooked her own meals, and hated the thought of having someone take care of her.

She'd lived in her house for fifty years. Until she decided to sell out, the house was going to stay put, and until she sold it, Zene didn't plan on going anywhere. He didn't need much space. He didn't know anyone to ask to dinner, and he wasn't going to decorate. His room had two simple functions—it gave him a closet for his suitcase and a dry spot to sleep in.

He started up the stairs, checked for mail on the table in the foyer. No mail. There hadn't been any yesterday. There wouldn't be tomorrow.

Mrs. Miller never talked to him about his mail. They were talking less all the time. Soon, there would be only silence between them. They had an understanding. He paid his rent. She never asked questions. He knew she'd tell him if the rent went up.

The house stank of fried onions and mildew. The carpet, old and red and worn, was a vestige of a time when people cared. Its hour had come and gone, and like the house, it was doing hard time until the wrecking ball slammed into it. A prisoner sentenced to live . . .

Zene clawed his way to the third floor. The stairs were good, solid stairs built by craftsmen who used the old tools for a clientele that knew what it wanted and wouldn't take anything less than quality. Plastic didn't just change the times, it changed people's heads.

At the top of the stairs from the room next door, Eddy Mortiboy and Zemda were shouting at each other over which TV program to watch. Zene wondered what could be worth fighting about at one-thirty in the morning. Swaying, he rapped on the door. The noise stopped.

Zene shoved open the unlocked door to his room. He didn't bother with a light. The curtainless window let in enough from the street for him to see where he was headed.

The room was simple. A table, a single wooden chair, a five-drawer dresser, and a double bed with a horseback sway in the middle.

Pulling his coat tight, Zene raised the window, then lay down on the bed with his boots on. The hollow in the mattress folded up over him like a tulip closing when the sun goes down. His head was fuzzy from the brew and the virus living in his body. The bartender's face as she kicked him out kept popping up through the fuzz—like the head on a glass of beer.

Cold air flooded through the window. Zene closed his eyes and crossed his arms over his chest.

A corpse in the morgue.

He stared at the ceiling, at the shadows on the wall, and listened to a motorcycle whine its way up Roosevelt.

Through the fog of his drunk, he saw himself cocooned, dread blooming in his head with the speed of a toxic mushroom.

Whittled down to the nub.

Not all the way down, but he was on the slope. One more bolt of bad luck and he would slide down to that place where having a room is a luxury. He'd been there more than once. It was always cold there when a man landed. He remembered one winter the day he was trying to hitch out of Lordsburg. A mechanic picked him up.

He took Zene to his house where he introduced his wife and his daughters. Zene figured something was wrong by the silence and the down-turned eyes at the dinner table. Later, the mechanic showed Zene the connubial bed, but the wife went to sleep with the daughters.

She knew her man.

She crept in silence without looking at Zene. She had a sweet deal—two daughters, no hope, and a husband who fucked vagrants. She looked the other way while her man plumped the sack for the bum who was going to pay for his room and board with flesh.

But Zene decided that he'd rather freeze in the Lordsburg cold than toast in the sheets with the mechanic. He left the guy sitting on the edge of the bed smoking a cheroot.

He met the wife in the hallway.

She wore a faded pink chenille housecoat, her hair sagging, arms folded under her breasts, cold, pleading history in her eyes.

You ain't gonna do nothin', are you?

No, you're carrying a load already.

He went back into the cold and found a truck stop where a guy hauling hay to Chama picked him up.

It was cold in Lordsburg. In Chama it was even colder.

There weren't that many unopened doors left. Zene had nailed the coffin lid shut on himself. He'd been out of work for eight months. His only assets were a driver's license with the chauffeur's endorsement, a thick beard, and an incurable case of misanthropy. Somehow, through everything, he'd kept his license. If the slide went on much longer, he would have to quit drinking.

That fear tore a gash in his breathing, and in the dark, he felt alone and dirty. Could a man implode? Disappear into himself. Invert his body and become nothing? It was tempting. Very tempting. Anything to keep from hitting bottom alone. That was the hard part, going all the way down with no one to know you were there.

Alfred

Alfred Von Stebbin looked like a wizened old man and there was nothing he could do about it. The men in his lineage aged fast from forty to fifty. For some people that was a timeless zone, like early childhood, when the differences were noticeable only to mothers. At fifty, Alfred was a wreck. His face and neck had wrinkled as though the meat had been sucked out of him, but his hands were the hands of a twenty-five-year-old that a malicious and vengeful god had grafted onto a wizened body.

A tall, thin Von Stebbin often reminded people of someone they had seen somewhere, maybe an aging and elegant character actor in domestic bliss films.

By thirty, his hair had gone from ink-black to salt-and-pepper grey. His moustache had turned bristle-grey.

Von Stebbin looked like a time-traveler stranded in a haberdashery selling second-hand knockoffs that had all the class of gunny sacks on a scarecrow. He teared up when he looked at himself in the mirror and saw the bones protruding through rusticated skin. Age was hard to take because Alfred knew that from fifty to eighty, his skin would not wrinkle more. A quirk of the genes. In twenty years, he would look the way he did at that moment. He had seen the pictures of his grandparents, his mother—ageless, his father—ancient.

Karizma

Karizma, Alfred's wife, hadn't aged in ten years. She was thirty-three. Every day they looked more like father and daughter. Alfred's grip on the eagle forced Karizma to buy ordinary clothes. She had buzz-cut her hair short in a style that young women liked as it birthed a sense of sexual ambiguity. She had a natural elegance and a sexual flair in the way she carried her body. It was the refined carriage of a courtesan who married money and turned seduction into cash before her teeth fell out. Alfred resented having to spend money on her, but he couldn't keep her caged up, and he wouldn't let her neglect her appearance. His plan was simple.

Make her disappear.

Watching Karizma eat dinner repulsed Von Stebbin. He detested everything about her—the way she chewed, the way she drank. He hated the way she dressed, the way she walked. He hated the unconscious, affected way she brushed at her cheek with the back of her hand when she talked.

In the beginning—beginnings are always fresh and true and wonderful—just after they were married, Alfred had been so eager to please her that he had made a fool of himself. For him at forty, her sexuality was an aphrodisiac. He had discovered her sex and his own needs at the same time, and there had been a lust-feast, weeks of it, until the scent of sex spread miasmic through the house, through the car. There was nothing he wouldn't have done for her so that she would do what he needed for himself. But she did not give him what he needed.

Because she failed in every way to satisfy him, he outgrew her as if she were a baggy pair of pants that no longer fit him.

He had underestimated the stupidity and the impatience of the young, and her inability to understand what he wanted and needed.

In the beginning, she'd been grateful and innocent. But there were parts of her she would not surrender to him, and those were the parts Alfred needed. There was a hard shell around the secret buried in her and nothing Alfred did got her to crack it open.

Trained as a scientist, Alfred understood rational thought and the empirical method, but he had betrayed science to lust.

He had fallen in love.

He had become body and now he was paying for betraying his mind. Aging, he had learned three important lessons—

You can't turn back time.

You can't remake human nature.

Young women don't want to be touched by men old enough to be their fathers unless that touch is golden.

Karizma was a selfish cow who ate his food, slept in his house, and taunted him with her skin and her hair and her legs, but refused, by choice, to relieve his frustrations.

Still, he had found ways to bend her to his needs.

Alfred knew Karizma slept with other men. He knew she gave them what she refused to give him. He knew that if he had been handsome, if he had been whiter, she might not have put distance between the two of them with her trysts. But respect did not substitute for money. He had learned too late that women, young women, don't marry for respect. They marry for love, they marry for money, they marry for security and adventure, but they don't marry for respect.

How does a man learn that lesson without having to live through the pain? Alfred's solution was simple enough—kill her.

But the law worried Alfred. He had to be careful. Any time the wife of a doctor or a dentist died, the police went crazy and the husband was always the first suspect.

Alfred wasn't going to get caught.

And then there were the divorce laws. Washington was a community property state. After ten years, Karizma was entitled to a share of what he had. The most important thing to him was to make sure that she didn't get it.

None of it.

If he'd had better business acumen, he'd have played with land or things which had a resale value. But he had let opportunities pass, and then one day, he realized that his marriage was failing, and if he now acquired things, whole portions of what he acquired would be hers. He spent hours imagining her hurt, destitute, stripped filthy-naked, and toothless, living on the street.

He wanted her gone from his life.

I need my allowance, Alfred.

Alfred looked at the source of the words. They had come from nowhere to interfere with his thoughts. He was lost, confused.

What?

I said, I need my allowance.

Come down to the office tomorrow.

Can't you write me a check tonight?

I didn't bring the checkbook.

Why do I have to beg, Alfred?

I'm not making you beg.

If this isn't begging, I don't know what is.

You should be thriftier.

How many ways can a person spend a dime?

It's not the dimes I'm worried about, it's the dollars.

I'm desperate.

How desperate?

You could let me have a bank card. They won't let you take money out unless you can cover it.

Checks are just fine.

If you want to eat tomorrow, I'll need some money.

He shoved himself away from the table, reached into his billfold and took out a twenty-dollar bill.

Will this cover it?

He rejoiced, watching anxiety rise up in her. He knew the knot tightening in her stomach, the nausea that preceded the rush of revulsion and fear.

Goddamn you, Alfred. Why do this to me?

I feed you, I clothe you, I provide housing and transportation for you. If you don't like the arrangement, you can always leave.

I won't give you that satisfaction, Alfred.

Then I'm afraid we cohabit this hornet's nest.

What about my allowance?

She stood, leaned on her end of the table, and glared at him.

You know the price of money.

You can't make me do that anymore.

You're free to choose.

There are bills. I need gas for my car. There's no soap for the dishwasher, I have to buy Tampax.

Alfred reveled in the anguish oozing out of her. It made him feel good to watch her squirm.

I'm going back to the office tonight. I've got some lab work waiting.

He pushed his chair under the table. She shoved the plate away from her—meatloaf and peas. He hated meatloaf. He knew she fixed it because he hated it. But soon, no more meatloaf.

Karizma

Karizma listened to the garage door close. Alfred backing his car into the street. He never returned before midnight. She dumped the meatloaf and the peas into the garbage, set the plates to soak in the sink, went upstairs to change.

She unbuttoned her blouse. Unzipped her skirt. Dropped them at the foot of the bed.

At the mirror, she inserted the dangly, gilded, sapphire earrings.

Lipstick. Fierce red. Eyeliner. Shadow.

She reached for the phone.

Charmaine, it's Kay, he's gone . . .

She dressed—black stockings, black spiked heels, a black leather miniskirt, a cobalt linen jacket. A peplum. Silver starburst buttons.

Under the leather miniskirt, naked skin.

On her way out of the house, she snatched the twenty off the table.

The car stopped at the curb. Karizma slid in. Charmaine kissed her on the cheek.

You look fabulous, hon. Did the old rat give you a hard time?

He knows I need money.

We've got a couple hot ones tonight, sweet. One of them asked for you again.

Does he have a name?

The Fat Guy—chipmunk cheeks.

Char, don't fuck around with me.

All he wants, baby, is that sweet ass of yours.

Oh god, Char, I'm such a mess.

You know you're doin' it right when they ask for you.

How much?

Enough.

In advance?

Charmaine patted a fuchsia, faux-leather purse on the seat of the Lincoln Town Car.

Envelope.

Not in the car, I hope.

The houseboat.

Karizma opened the purse, opened the envelope, counted ten one-hundred dollar bills, then sealed the envelope.

I just don't like it in the car.

Zene

Then came morning, and with morning came the thunder inside his skull.

Early mornings, thunder always came from inside his skull.

Thunder and pain running through bone and blood.

He lay still until the ache in his bladder shouted get up. He didn't want to, but it was get up or piss in the mattress. He wasn't ready to sleep again in his own urine, but he didn't want to get up and cross that floor to that bathroom because he would have to move his head.

If he pissed in the mattress, Mrs. Miller would find out. Would she evict him? He had a choice. It wasn't much of a choice. But it was one of the few choices left for him.

He got up. Thunder. Pain.

The house was silent.

The air was stale.

His hands hurt. Patches of skin torn out of the heel of his right hand. He looked at his hand, and an engram from the beer-night flashed through the thunder tearing through his brain. He hadn't hit anyone. He hadn't talked to anyone.

He had fallen.

He had fallen down.

Bathroom. Down the hall.

His urine, thick. Smelled of decay and dying. Smelled the way beer smelled after it filtered through his kidneys, his brain, his heart, his blood.

Back in his room, he searched the top dresser-drawer, but he stopped.

What was he looking for?

What was he waiting for?

The thunder boomed again in his head—the death knell, the sound of death-bells announcing his sinking into the darkness again. Again the bells. The headache.

Aspirin.

He was looking for aspirin while he awaited the scythe. Both aspirin and the guillotine were guaranteed to stop the pain.

He wanted aspirin, but what he needed was a slug of mad dog, a quart of Red Hook, a pint of rye. But he had nothing. No aspirin. In time, the headache would wear itself out, the guillotine poised over his neck stall out, the scythe, half-swung, staying in its arc, waiting for another day to finish its fall.

On the dresser, a quart jar of Sunny Jim peanut butter, a half loaf of Bread Garden 12 grain bread, an economy size jar of strawberry jam, and a jar of instant coffee—Mexican. On the table, a box of C&H sugar, a portable, single-cup water-heating element.

Zene hooked a cracked mug on his finger, and back in the bathroom, filled the cup.

The heater was the extent of his cooking. He plugged in the coil and plunged it into the water.

Waiting for water to boil, Zene smeared peanut butter on a single slice of bread and spread a thin covering of strawberry jam on the peanut butter.

Bubbles formed on the heating element. Hot water. Instant coffee.

He stirred in two spoons of sugar.

At the window, he sipped the coffee and stood looking at the world.

Another day full of sweat, fatigue, and bad memories—the residue of the virus that had eaten his brain.

To the West, beyond the city and the Sound, the Olympics jutted up, white, tall, distant. The mountains were mountains. In the thirty-three years he'd been looking at them, they hadn't moved. They weren't going away.

When he looked at them, he didn't see ideas, he didn't see dreams, he saw mountains. He saw rock and dirt and snow.

Mountains. Pure. Trees. Water. Animals. Deer. No humans. Trees without humans, the world before human flesh corrupted it.

But the city—the city that had cut him into pieces and chewed his mind, his bone, his future—lay spread out silent and beautiful and poisonous, and deep in the concrete canyons, the kitchens of hate boiled men and women, turned them into jelly, served them up in glops on marble tables where tycoons born naked ate the underlings with silver fork and knife, laughing as they gnawed the tasteless meat.

Zene had been there. Dinner. On their table. More than once. He had no chance now. He had no connections now. He had no way to break into the palaces of money. He stood outside now— they had won.

He glanced at his watch—an elaborate electronic timepiece, a chronometer they called it, that could do everything but speak Chinese. It read 6:17 a.m., and the date was 8. You knew the month. Zene liked its terse eloquence. Death was there at some hour, somewhere.

His hands trembled.

Not yet the DTs telling him he had to quit drinking.

He took a deep breath. Quit drinking? Why?

He'd go for a couple weeks pouring booze into his gut like every other addict, and then, one day the need and the urge and the promise of oblivion went silent and the hole opening up to the underworld closed and he'd stop.

Drinking.

Today, the library. No bar. No beer. No Patty with the weaponized bar towel.

He finished his Mexican coffee and went out into the grey, cold, sterile Seattle morning.

His breath misted as he walked. The library. When he wasn't drinking, he was reading. When he wasn't reading, he was walking. When he wasn't walking, he drank. Anything to crush the vision of unbeing rising out of the pages he read in books.

At the Lake City branch, at the university branch, some days he walked to Greenwood where an eager, young librarian said hello even when he didn't reply, but went silent to read.

She knew what he was doing, she never made trouble for him.

He liked that. The aging librarians were hens fluttering when a homeless fox curled up in a hard, wooden chair and he didn't like that. He needed to be alone. He wanted to be alone. Why did he need to be alone?

When he couldn't sit still long enough to read, he walked. Since he had sold his car, he walked the city, walked miles, looking. Just looking.

Selling the Volvo wasn't a good idea. When his boots wore out, he'd have to pick up another pair at Sir Plus in the University District. He shoved his hands into his pockets and came up with one glove.

Left glove.

How to cope with one glove? He slipped it on and stuck his right hand in his coat pocket. The coat was a down-filled, Arctic parka he got from Saint Vincent. It was a good coat for the rain.

At the 24/7 on the corner of Roosevelt and 92nd, he stopped. In the window, on a hunk of cardboard, a sign—

We're Hiring.

In the store, behind the counter—Marshawn Casey.

Marshawn Casey

Marshawn Casey was a huge chunk of man with a huge laugh, shoulders forged out of cast-iron, and hands big enough to haul two boys and a small ox. On the ring finger of his right hand, he wore a special ring that told where he had been. His past, as a defensive tackle on the best eleven the 'Hawks had ever fielded, lived on in the love-glow of fandom, but football had broken parts of him that showed as shadows in the X-rays. X-rays didn't register the pain.

Zene liked Casey because he knew Casey's pain. His size masked a good, big man who had achieved perfection until the bones showed him the exit. He was not like white Americans who'd gone through the public school system bathed in a neurotic need to be liked, coupled with a morbid fear of rejection. Football had shown him the light of a physical truth that he now hid behind a beard and a thick layer of gruffness. If you knew where to look, you saw Casey's hurt, and Zene saw it. He looked for that part of Casey he found in himself.

About the sign.

What about it?

I might be looking for a job.

You look like you might of been sleeping in your clothes.

You nailed it.

You look like a bum.

Clear away the crap and you'll find a gold-plated prince.

What's a prince doing rustling me for a job?

I was driving a bus and now I'm not because they fired me and I been on a toot the last couple weeks.

Why'd they fire you?

I told my supervisor to "go shove it." They called it "gross insubordination," and then they fired me.

That's all?

I hit him.

I like your logic. You talk with your fists and you're looking for a job in a place where people don't give you nothin' but lip. You don't have a snowball's chance in hell . . .

I can do stuff.

Like what?

Add and subtract. Think. Do long division. Read and write. I can even tell my ass from a hole in the ground.

You got a leg up on most of the idiots who walk in here, then. You ever ran a cash register?

Grew up on one.

I'll bet.

In fifteen minutes, Zene had talked himself into a job. The thing that sealed it was when he told Casey he lived just down the street.

So, if you can't drag your lazy ass to work, I know where to find you.

No. If I don't come to work, that's the last place you'll find me.

You got more clothes than those rags you been sleeping in?

Somewhere.

The beard's gotta go.

You've got a beard.

My six-six carries three hundred pounds and it's my store.

Yeah, the beard gives you that venerable look, but I've got a weak chin.

Like hell you do. I know when I see a killer lined up against me, so okay, keep the beard, but keep it trimmed and keep it clean. No spaghetti sauce. I hate beards with spaghetti sauce.

I don't eat Italian.

PayDay

It was a clerkship that paid a few cents above minimum wage, and he'd work the graveyard shift. The shift of the living dead. Zene trained with the day clerk and went to work that night.

It wasn't the zoo he thought it would be. A few deviants who couldn't afford computers came in to look at the magazines with naked women in them.

The rule was you buy Marshawn Casey's magazines, you didn't stand around and perv out on his dime.

Others came in high, couldn't remember why they were there, and left with a quart of milk.

Most of the trade after midnight meant business. They didn't want to talk or cause trouble, they wanted to get in and get out and do something productive, like rub off one and go to sleep in the afterglow.

The Washington State lottery shot up to four million, and while Zene didn't move much bread, he shuffled lottery tickets out the door by the truckload. Every night.

At four million, the perverts lost interest in the nudie magazines. Four million taters could buy a lifetime of straight perv.

For the first time since Mexico, Zene trimmed his beard. He washed his hair in the sink in the restroom of Marshawn Casey's 24/7.

He felt good.

Casey paid half in cash and half in check, and that was fine with Zene. Casey treated him like he was human, and Zene kind of liked it. He liked Marshawn Casey.

He liked the idea of buying a new pair of gloves.

With his first payday, he paid his rent.

He talked to Mrs. Miller about the weather and the travesty of leftist politics in the state and the country. Mrs. Miller, a legacy WOBBLY, said she was convinced that the left were a dying breed. Zene told her he wasn't sure. She said look at the collapse of communism. Zene told her it would come back when greed-driven, pernicious, predatory capitalism failed. She said she'd been waiting for fifty years. It's like prostate cancer, Zene told her, it takes a long time for it to go lethal.

He bought gloves, new socks, and fresh jars of coffee, peanut butter, and jam. He had money left. He was ready for the collapse.

By the beginning of the second week, he was enjoying the nighttime circus. No winner for the lottery. It kicked up to five million. Five million brought out the lost ones who bet their milk money on the come.

The nights rolled by smooth until the night she stepped through the door.

Karizma

Her name was Karizma Carlson, and she was born with a full set of teeth. Once in a galaxy far away, Zene had asked her to the Roosevelt High School Senior Prom. Fifteen years of hopelessness later, she walks in and he's a worm in a barnyard full of hungry chickens.

He pretended not to know her when she laid the pack of Dunhill Lights on the counter under a five-dollar bill.

Zene made change, shoved it back to her, avoided eye contact, but she smiled a faint flicker of recognition, followed by years of what-the-hell.

The beard.

He turned to another customer.

Karizma pocketed the Dunhills.

When she was gone, Zene tried to light a cigarette, but his fingers turned to Play-Doh and he flicked the lighter twice, then dropped the weed on the floor and crushed it with the heel of his boot.

He dreaded running into people he knew from the old days. There was always somebody who wanted to dig into his world of lost dreams. Zene wasn't interested in lost dreams. He wasn't interested in much, but for sure he didn't want to talk about old times with a woman who had given him stone aches relieved only with self-abuse.

In the time he was driving the bus, no one ever recognized him. That was because of the uniform. A guy in a bus driver's uniform doesn't exist from the neck up. A bus driver is the fleshy part of the machine—a faceless bone-and-blood ticket-taker, a talking street map. In a place like Casey's 24/7, you didn't hide behind a uniform.

Clerks have faces, and the first thing customers see is face. Faces with eyes feasting on him. Being seen was like being cut, but no one saw the blood or the skeleton of anguish. Zene squirmed when he saw his past creep through the door. He was selling burritos and corn chips and lottery tickets. He wasn't selling condos or houses to women with kids and dogs. He wasn't selling expensive vacations by rivers in the sunshine. Corn chips. Burritos.

He tried to shove Karizma out of his mind, but she stuck there, glued there, a taste of what might have been—that skin, those lips, that hair. Wrapped up in memory, Zene shorted a woman on her change, a woman he hadn't noticed standing at the counter until she tapped a fifth of bourbon on the counter.

Sorry ma'am, old age getting to the grey matter.

Yeah, sure.

Old Times

On Saturday night, the state announced the lottery winners on TV. The store was empty. Karizma Carlson came in. Zene was alone. No avoiding her.

Zene?

It was half a question wrapped up in a half-statement. She'd gotten a fix on him. He wanted to crawl into the trash can under the counter, but he stayed on his feet.

Do I owe you money?

He was weak. He was going to implode. He pulled out a cigarette. Vacant, he'd made a wrong turn on the dirt road to hell.

Zene, come on, high school? Karizma Carlson . . .

Right. Now I got it. English, right?

Algebra. Spanish . . .

Sure, algebra with Ms. Izokaitis, the Lithuanian refugee . . .

You work here?

Midnight to eight.

Zene wanted her to go away. But she didn't. She wasn't runway chic, but she hadn't been sleeping with the Wallingford Troll. Lush as a ripe strawberry, she stood looking at him.

Then she smiled and left.

Zene felt like she'd kicked him in the nuts and tossed him down a dark hole. She'd read him the way a hungry man reads a garbage can at Wendy's. In thirty seconds, she knew everything about him—down to his sock size and the waistband on his thirty-two-waist jockeys. He wanted to slither out the door and never come back. There were a million reasons to get out of Seattle and she was number one.

But there was one thing that kept him planted in place—she still set his brain on fire, turned up the heat in his gonadal thermostat until his boiler red-lined. She was gone, but his head clouded up like he was in the first half-hour of a sweet wine drunk that got worse the longer he nipped at the juice.

After his shift, he went to bed where he lay awake studying the ceiling while he cataloged everything from the minute she had walked into the store to his last cigarette. Her eyes—surprised, anxious—had tracked him. He was a small rodent in a raptor's claws. She had picked up her change in slender fingers, bright red, polished nails. And the hair. Her hair still had that shiny, black glint of spilled oil, but now it was cropped and cut cute. The hair was short, but the gesture hadn't changed in fifteen years—she reached up with the back of her hand, the way a woman does when she has grease on her fingers, or her hands were wet with lube—and brushed at her cheek.

When Zene closed his eyes, she floated, a black-and-white hologram stuck in the glue of memory, suspended in time.

Zene.

The first time in fifteen years she had spoken his name and it made him shudder. What would it be like with her? He drifted on a vibrating stream of images and forget—forgetting who and what he was until desire dynamited his loins. The hologram transmogrified into a film running in his mind—pictures of her flashed across his inner eye, but she wasn't a face, she was a body with black hair and long legs spread wide, and Zene went numb.

His head went numb.

His lips went numb.

His hands went numb.

His tongue went numb, and he was seventeen-numb again, and she had kissed him off the night before the prom and he was nothing.

What could come of it? Nothing. Nothing.

What would Mrs. Miller say if she knew he was lying in her house, in her bed running a private porno about fucking a woman he hadn't smelled or seen or touched in fifteen years?

Hands behind his head, Zene forced his mind back into numbness, back into nothingness—arm-wrestling with her image until Karizma Carlson seeped away the way air leaks from a balloon, leaving him with acute gonadal emptiness that he had stopped payment on fifteen years ago.

When the numbness reached his feet, he lay suspended in his own nothingness—a man with no name, floating in warm, salty nothing.

The stillness in his austere room crushed him—the absolute and utter quietness of being alone in a universe so dead that sound was only an echo in memory.

Tangled in her memory, he fell asleep. When he woke up, his bladder was full, and it was two hours till his next shift.

Monica

Alfred had been in the lab for an hour when he heard the click in the outer office. He moved his stool closer to the bench. He felt the door open. Felt the quick splash of air loaded with the thick scent of her.

Expectation made him light-headed.

The steps closed in on him, but he didn't turn. He fingered the instruments on the bench.

She stood behind him—quiet, redolent, perfumy—for a long time. He caught his breath. Her breath cascaded into him, a mountain crushing him.

He looked at the wall in front of him. His shadow merged with Monica Duncan's shadow—a grotesque, amorphous being that was both of them and neither of them.

Her fingers settling on his neck with the gentleness of a butterfly on a flower. She gripped his shoulders. He shuddered. His cock hardened. He loved that feeling, impossible of late, that hard cock of a man with woman on his mind and her scent in his nose. Another fractured breath.

With the heels of her hands, Monica massaged the muscles of his neck, then his scalp, with her fingertips.

Possessing him.

Alfred turned on the stool, slow, everything slow now, perfume slow, slow sweat, slow, hard breath, and he slow-buried his face in her belly, circled her hips with his arms, the odor of her body stiffening his cock until his staggered breath left him lightheaded—again.

The slick fabric of her uniform cool against his cheek. He swam in the gentle rise and fall of her breathing. He pulled her closer, her odors, her perfume, her body heat.

He looked up.

Her face glowing.

The whiteness of her uniform, the blackness of her hair, turned her into an angel of evil, exuding sex and the odors of sex, and the smell stormed inside him until he surrendered.

He surrendered.

He touched her nipples, plump under the thin uniform material. The zipper of her dress was down to her navel. He was weak.

You came back.

Do you want me to leave?

She bent over him, ran her hands over his cheeks and kissed him. He melted into the scent rising from her skin.

She was her usual bitchy-self tonight.

Shut up.

She unzipped the dress, opened her nakedness to him.

Oh, Jesus.

Suck.

And he did.

Monica stepped back into her panties, tucked her breasts back into the uniform, ran her fingers through her sparking, black hair.

Alfred loved that motion. It said everything about her.

The first time he had seen her do that was the day she applied for the job. He knew then, by the musky odor of her body, that he would sleep with her. He had hired her that day. A week later, she returned to the office for the first time after work. When she left, she was no longer just an employee. Her scent on his hands was new and sharp, the taste of her in his mouth a smooth poison.

Alfred knew he had started a new phase in his life.

She's got a nasty mouth and all she wants is my money.

She's your wife, Al, of course she wants money.

She pursed her lips as she looked in the mirror.

I don't like having to do it this way, sugar. Why can't we go to your place . . .?

You know why.

No one knows me there.

And we'll keep it that way.

I'm not sure we're doing the right thing.

Don't you love me?

You know I do.

I have a price, Al . . . The first night you sleep in my bed will cost you.

I can't. She'd clean me out.

Then you can't sleep in my bed, can you?

Monica, this doesn't make sense.

It makes perfect sense to me.

It isn't easy.

You get what you want, don't you?

Not everything.

How many of us do, darling?

How can you be so kind and patient and she's such a slut?

How do you expect me to answer that?

She sat down on the stool and spun around. He watched the mesmerizing, full-breasted Amazon in front of him. Wide hips. Narrow waist. Lean, muscular legs that held him inside her when he came.

She spun, smiling at him each time she came around, her shadow moving on the wall as she turned and turned and turned.

It was after two when Alfred pulled his BMW into the garage. Karizma's car was in its place. He felt the hood. Cold. He padded upstairs, stopping outside her door, but heard nothing. He didn't try the knob. She always locked it.

In the stale closeness of his own room, the scent of the other woman heavy in his mouth, he licked his fingers, sucked her remains into him. He wanted to sleep with her smell in him.

He lay on his cot, his hands fluttering over his crotch. He rose again, rigid with the memory of her. He ate her scent, swallowed her remains, chewing on the odor her body left in his hands.

He caught his breath.

Coming into his hand.

It took so little to make him happy.

Karizma. If she had cared just a bit, he could have forgiven her everything.

Hot Water

Monica Duncan stood, eyes closed, letting the water scald her body until she turned a bright, painful pink. She liked the water so hot the pain was one notch below agony, then, coming, she hit the cold and the sudden burst was a flail, snapping her. Skin numb after the sting of a scourge, she eased the water back to body temperature. Adjusted the shower head to heavy pulse.

Water beat on her face and neck, and she bent over to let the stream of water pound at the small of her back. When the stream cooled, she got out and dried with a heavy, terry-cloth towel.

She pulled off the shower cap. She wiped the mirror. She shook her hair out. The black hair curled to her shoulders. She finished drying, then studied her figure in the mirror. She liked what she saw. She was thirty-eight. Her face still firm, no lines around the eyes. The arched eyebrows framed black eyes, her lips echoed the lines of the brows. Her breasts were large and heavy. The look of pseudo-pregnancy gave her a ripe, delicious aura. The full-bodied woman looking back at her in the glass was very much in control of herself and the situation she had created.

She ran her fingers through her hair, she thought of Alfred. It wouldn't be long.

Monica had been born with insights into human weakness for reading character and nailing down the frustration that tied men in knots. With the wisdom of a madam in a whorehouse, she read the man and knew his kinks and perversions—Head. Mouth. Ass. She knew everything about Alfred, and through him, a lot about Karizma. Three months of working for Alfred, she had him confessing his peccadillos and his fantasies, including the tortures and pain he needed to inflict on a woman. Sometimes she indulged him. She had known larger.

Alfred now would do anything she wanted. His impatience showed, but she didn't want to hurry him. It would happen. His hesitation made it easier and holding him at bay excited her. If it took too long, she would rethink her plan. So much could go wrong with revenge. She wanted things to break down the middle.

Monica saw Alfred as a man ripe for revenge, because he, like every man, was a monster with two personalities.

Two Alfreds

When he was alone, Alfred was a different man than when he was with patients. Alone, he walked with a shuffle, shoulders bent, head down, but when he was with patients, the second Alfred Von Stebbin emerged—the professional with the miraculous touch. Soft hands administered lidocaine without traumatizing the patient. An artist with the drill. Even people who dreaded the chair found themselves at ease under his skill.

He was disciplined in his work, and he never thought about suicide. He was an excellent dentist, who, through self-denial and rigor, got beyond his personal hatred of his profession when he was practicing it.

Discipline was his inheritance from a time when you didn't talk about property, and money was something others suspected you had but never asked how much. Alfred learned dentistry at the University of Washington School of Dentistry. Discipline became part of him—like breathing and his hair color. Monica needed that Alfred and she had him hooked.

Monica

Alfred didn't ask for references when Monica applied for the job. Temps had filled the position for a month. Alfred was ready for any competent person to step in and take over. The signs of sin were there the day Karizma came into the office and Monica mistook her for Alfred's daughter. Monica hired a detective who followed Karizma. By the end of the week, Monica knew more about Karizma's proclivities, her sins, and her dreams than Alfred ever would. And what she found, she liked.

Karizma had Luciferian blood in her.

Monica knew Karizma's brand of rebellion. She needed to flaunt it the way a teenager flaunts her nascent sexuality. Monica understood the psychology of young girls whose fathers wanted to possess them. It had made her work on Alfred so easy, but Monica didn't yet know what it would take to push Alfred into murder. The answer was in how much he loved her. Some people kill because they love too much. Some kill because they cannot love. Monica knew Alfred was a killer because Karizma was hurting him. But the monk in Alfred was such that he enjoyed the flail. Karizma's infidelities were a form of flagellation, and the scourge was other men's penises. Alfred wrapped himself in abuse and bowed his back as Karizma skinned him raw.

That was fine with Monica. Things were moving right along.

Smelling of lemon shampoo, skin flushed with heat, rich with a scented deodorant, Monica padded naked into the bedroom and sat down at the computer. A first-class machine. She had spent to get it, but it was the machine she needed to make things work. She switched on the printer, called up Publisher, loaded a file, and adjusted the form that appeared on the screen.

She worked for fifteen minutes, then printed the document. It came off the LaserJet looking like a professional print job. She then rolled the invoice into the ancient IBM Selectric typewriter that sat on the desk beside the computer. In comparison to the high-powered electronic equipment, the typewriter was noisy and slow. She filled in the blanks in the invoice, put the invoice in an envelope, addressed the envelope to Alfred Von Stebbin, DDS, and put a stamp on it. It would arrive at the office in a day or two, looking very much like a legitimate billing for building maintenance. The amount due was $1,003.52.

Her Pet

Iqbal lay naked on the sheet, on his back, his chocolate-brown body lean as good bacon. His mouth a cinnamon slit glittering with white teeth. Sitting astride him, Monica ran her hands between his legs. Iqbal clamped her hand in his thighs.

You always work late, Monica.

His speech was accented with clipped, retroflex Urdu consonants.

Dr. Von Stebbin is a busy man.

I'm coming there to see exactly what you do for him.

Do you want to fuck me, Iqbal, or argue about an old man?

He should pay you more if you have to do technical work.

Go back home, Iqbal, go to your sweet little woman.

You say every month he'll give you a raise, but no raise.

I'm ready, Iqbal.

He sank his teeth into her breast. Monica did not flinch, she did gasp as the sliver of pain loosened her wetness. Iqbal rolled her onto her stomach.

They lay fitted together—two tiles in a tessellated design. She liked having him mount her from behind. His first shyness disappeared as she taught him what pleased her, what made her come. He grew into it and now he clung to her back the way a small, squeaking animal mounts its mother.

Monica made him sweat. Sweat washed away the memory of Alfred's bony fingers probing her. Iqbal rode her hard, dripped on her back, and dripping, rode her harder, rode her until he, rigid, drowned in his pleasure and gave in to the little death that bound him to her, made him grateful to her, and she, she needed the scent of his semen to bring her to the edge, and she clenched, holding him inside her, his hands swimming over her, his weight pressing her down.

Twenty-four/Seven

Zene looked up as the door opened and Karizma floated in with a tall, white woman whose fuchsia hair framed her face. She had an aquiline nose and sharp, angular, vulturesque cheek bones. The two of them were enough to make a man wish he had been born wired for 220.

Karizma bought her pack of Dunhills, but didn't introduce her friend, who, in her red jacket, looked hard and tired enough to be a model.

When they walked out, Zene watched legs all the way into the car. The vulture drove. She looked both ways when she pulled out of the lot. Numbness seeped first into Zene's feet, then to his hand, then into his head, and he was dead. Karizma was an injection of high potency xylocaine. His brain had stopped working.

The numbness wasn't permanent, but it did last long enough for death to creep into his brain. When it wore off, Zene got back to punching the cash register.

Karizma.

Her fuchsia-haired friend. Dressed up to prowl, maybe drinking, maybe up at the Maple Leaf Grill or down at the Far Side at the bottom of the hill. No, she wouldn't go to the Far Side dressed like that. The Far Side was a rock bar with loud guitars and young girls in miniskirts, no underwear girls, girls who were just learning how to grease their equipment.

Maybe she drank at Cooper's. Zene thought thoughts about her that he didn't want to think, so he washed his hands in the sink, then sold half-a-dozen lottery dreams to half-a-dozen faceless, nameless creatures with bad breath and no hope.

Five Thousand, Four Hundred, Seventy-Five Days

In high school, in the deep despair of teenage weltschmerz, Zene had gawked at Karizma, dreamed of her black, braided hair, hard, black hair that was different from the cheerleader blonds who flashed their butts on Friday nights. No. Karizma held herself proud and at ease in her own skin. Zene was so aware of her that sometimes he hurt just looking at her. He had tried to talk to her, once, as they waited for English class to start, but his tongue stayed glued to the roof of his mouth and pure, prime nonsense spewed out of him. As far as he knew, no one ever asked her out. Maybe because she was formidable, maybe because she was tall. She wasn't like other girls with top-tier boyfriends who went to other schools where they majored in superiority.

He spent three-and-a-half years hiding a permanent erection behind his books when he walked out of class after her.

And then, one day, he stopped her in the hallway after class and in a spontaneous act, spouted words of self-destruction that sounded like a pidgin of two unknown languages, asked her to the senior prom.

She raised her hand to brush away hair that had not strayed from the cornrows and said yes before he'd even finished.

He didn't know which was worse, accepting or rejecting.

It didn't matter because the night before the prom, she called to say she couldn't make it.

He'd rented a white sport coat and set it up to share a limo with a friend. But she backed out and he'd been empty for a long time, feeling the kind of pain that only an adolescent who's just cracked his shell and gotten stomped on knows. Did she say no because he was white?

She didn't come to class after that. He learned that she'd dropped out. He never saw her again. The pain didn't go away until he learned about women who said yes whether there was money on the dresser or not.

Then, fifteen years older, he discovered that the salve soothing the rawness of despair wasn't very thick. Nothing had changed. He was old and she was killer-beautiful, and she made him hurt. A hundred other women in twenty cities had failed to kill that ache. The deeper part of him told the deep part of him that he didn't know her.

Not at all.

Not really.

But it didn't matter.

He was in love.

He was sinking fast in the hole that was fifteen-years deep and so lost in those fifteen years that he didn't come back to the time of plague until an old woman with no mask, toothless, stumbled in, waving a handful of dollar bills and muttering to herself. Her name was Molly, and she spent her social security money on lottery tickets. She counted the bills out, one by sweaty one, and blithered on about her odds of winning a million bucks. Zene told her that the odds were the same whether she bought tickets or not. What would she do with five million dollars if she won? Five million? Son of a bitch. She cackled at him and disappeared into the night, like all dreamers already spending money they'd never see.

And Then

Karizma came in alone. It hurt him to look at her. She had painted her thick lips a cruel bright red. She wore a yellow sweatshirt that had Chinese calligraphy silk-screened on it. A gold chain hung from her neck. On the chain, a pendant lay between her breasts. Tight, white jeans. Zene glanced at the pendant. A ring with a diamond in it.

She surprised him by hanging around, relaxed, talking at him. He didn't ask where she lived. He told her nothing she didn't already know about him. Her words spilled over him, half-drowning him, half-smothering him, leaving him feeling helpless and stupid and numb, leaving him behind in a pool of dripping words.

Shift Changes

The day the swing-shift woman quit to go to work for Microsoft, Marshawn went over the crazy-cliff.

Goddamn, Zene, is everybody in the whole goddamned city going to work for Microfuckingsoft? What they got going over there, anyway?

I don't know, Marshawn, but maybe you oughta buy some of it and put it in the store.

Marshawn had other things eating at him. He couldn't find a reliable body to handle swing shift. Did Zene mind filling in both shifts for a couple days, maybe a week? Maybe a month? Maybe longer? No, Zene didn't mind, he could use the extra loot and what if She came in again without her built-like-a-model white friend with ruin written deep in her perversion?

Alone, it was a ritual—Karizma Carlson dropped by for her Dunhills alone, and she'd talk about the weather or the lottery, and then leave.

When she was with the ruined woman, she was business. Smokes. In. Out.

Zene looked forward to her solo visits.

He placed bets with himself as to the time she'd come in. Every day she showed up, he was more comfortable with her. He knew that somewhere down the line, her visits had stopped being commercial.

Days she didn't come in, he thought about her, thought about how it would be with her, thought about what he had missed fifteen years ago, but he didn't think about her naked—no, not now—he did think about her skin and her eyes, her face and her neck, and her hands that floated soft and dark, and he imagined the touch of those hands on his skin.

She didn't make him feel like slime and she didn't try to grind him down with sly looks and that superior, ruining tone of voice, the superior tone of voice that puts a servant in his place, a tone that's sharper than a fang.

Karizma took him as he was. She would leave and he couldn't remember what they'd talked about, but he always had a nice feeling, the same feeling he got after two beers on a sunny afternoon.

No Show

The Saturday night she didn't come in, Zene waited. He punched cash register keys, looked at his watch, watched the street.

Abandoned.

All swelled up and nothing to do with it except dream.

Sunday, the same thing.

She skipped six days—he counted—before he resented it. He wasn't ready for the anger and hurt that her absence ripped out of him. Senior prom angst without a white sport coat. Just when he was getting used to her, she disappeared.

History repeating itself.

Maybe she was the goddess of eternal misery.

Monday

He lost control of his misery as it morphed into depression, then into despair, but he was glad it had ended only with a broken heart instead of a deep dive into death. What could have come of it?

She was married, probably rich, at least not hurting, and here he was hawking Tampax and candy bars. There were people who bought BMWs by selling candy bars and Tampax, but they didn't do it one at a time.

Zene and Marshawn Casey were getting along—Zene was doing the job, he wasn't stealing except for an occasional Big Gulp. Casey liked the way Zene handled himself.

I'm building up my reserves.

Layin' in good for doomsday?

No, feeling good enough to think about buying a car, but the ads sing a different song.

Don't get too deep.

Never more than waist-deep, Marshawn.

You quit drinking?

Only on days that start with B.

Casey told him he was a funny guy, but he still had to work.

The car. They had changed the state law so that you had to have car insurance. Insurance ran the cost of a car over the edge for Zene and his DUI wasn't going to help, so he stopped dreaming.

Why buy a car?

Where was he going?

He had entered an age of limits, anyway. Cut back, save, reuse, recycle, buy cheap, hunt the bargain, never pay full price. The world, going cheap, was using itself up. The ice caps were melting, sea level rising, the forests dying, and people still wanted the cheapest Brazilian beef burger with extra fries.

When Zene went to double shifts, Casey let him eat at the store. That was good. Zene's food budget dropped ten pounds—no hamburgers, no pizza—and his savings account put on weight. He wasn't drinking and that was good. It was always good to cut back the drinking, but there weren't that many reasons to do it. Money was one, but even money had its limits.

Tuesday night, a couple of stoned teenagers came in to practice their shoplifting. One of them pulled a six pack of Henry's and a pack of Camels. Zene wanted to see some ID, and while they argued about it, the other kid stuffed candy bars and burritos—everything except Eskimo Bars—into his coat pockets.

When he looked like the Pillsbury Doughboy, he sauntered past the register.

No ID, no beer.

Fuck you, old man.

The two thieves hit the door at the same time. Zene collared the Pillsbury Doughboy and told him to dump his load right there. It wasn't Zene's style to have pimple-poppers arrested. His style was knocking them around, taking their pelf, booting them out, sending them home to shave their peach-fuzz and come back the next day without blood on their chins to apologize.

But these two didn't buckle. It took Zene a second to see what they were up to. They were big boys who weren't scared of much. It was like they had planned to smear some hard time on Zene's face and smother it with ketchup. One of them shoved him into the glass door while the other kicked him. Zene went down but came up swinging.

He took turns bleeding them from busted lips and crunched noses before they hurtled backwards into the street. Zene didn't care that they were teenagers, all he saw was black and blood and blue, and his fists didn't hurt, but the boys felt it and damn did Zene love the smell of ripped flesh and the sound of a fist crunching an eyeball.

The alarm was going crazy by the time the cops got there. Zene had the two teenage hotshots by the short hair, feeding them knuckleburgers.

The cops pulled him off. The boys were broken. They thought they were tough, but they'd never seen rage. They didn't know that when a man alone has nothing to live for, he sees dying as an excuse to chop Homo sapiens sapiens down to the bone and grind his meat.

Zene was assessing his personal damage when a ranting Marshawn showed up.

You crazy son-of-a-bitch, you think with your knuckles, you goddamned chowder head.

The cop told him what had happened—

These two been terrorizing convenience stores in the North End for the last month, so it's good your guy iced them.

Marshawn backpedaled to safer ground and apologized to Zene in a tongue-twisting, zigzag of *mea culpas*, but he couldn't give Zene the rest of the night off because he had a hot sleeve on deck back at a party so he called a cab and closed the shop and paid for Zene's stitches at the Northwest hospital emergency room.

The next day, Marshawn told Zene to take a two-day vacation, and when he came back, he was going permanent on swing shift, because he'd found a woman crazy enough to work graveyard.

Her old man is a cop. She packs and don't run from shit.

I don't care, Marshawn.

Well, you oughta, you oughta care about your fellow workers. What the hell are we if we don't care about our crew?

All right. I care. I really care.

That's better. I like it all my employees like each other. It makes for like a small family, you know. You look like hell, Zene.

I was born that way, Marshawn.

Zene took his wages, paid his rent, and found a stool at the Maple Leaf Grill where he softened his scabs with steins of Red Hook.

Ma Schudie

The Maple Leaf Grill had gone through enough personality changes to make Robin Williams think about switching professions. Zene had been a stranger there since Ma Schudie's offspring sold it.

For years, Ma Schudie ran the neighborhood tavern that no one went to, but it didn't matter because she didn't need money. She had lived in the back and during the day sat in a wooden rocking chair in the window and looked out at the world passing by on Roosevelt.

Traffic was most of the movement in her life.

The Grill was a quiet place where you could go and sit and get tanked without emptying your wallet. Ma Schudie had been too blind to care and too old to worry, so, your glass empty, you refilled it yourself from the gallon jug she kept in the cooler. One brand for all—a Thunderbird-type of wine without the skid row class.

When you left, you dropped your money in the open till and Ma Schudie nodded. At one point, business had declined to where only Zene and a few hardened veterans of the white wine wars paid her much attention. Then, Ma Schudie died.

The new owners were mid-capitalist, fascists with only a touch of predatory plutocracy. They remodeled the kitchen, put in draft beer, and hired a chef. You used to sit for hours and think about what might have been, but now they played noise on a Bose system while young women named Cyndi and Tabetha took orders for Ballard Bitters and Rat City Ale and potato skins with nacho sauce.

Karizma

Zene sat nursing a nostalgia for the good old days when Karizma walked in bringing a primeval frost that ran straight through his gonads and up into his brain and he wanted to ignore her, but it was hard to ignore lightning in a red dress and high heels.

She plucked a pack of Dunhills out of her purse, and, still standing, lit one. Zene made room as she mounted a stool beside him and said nothing, and they sat for two cuts of sad music by sadder singers while sucking clouds of silence until Cyndi took Karizma's order with a smile singing on lips that had probably never kissed anything but lips.

Karizma, her mouth as red as poisoned raspberries, settled in with a glass of rosé and took her time worrying it dry.

Zene stared into his beer.

You think I'm a beachball, you chasing me around?

I'm not chasing you.

Zene watched her hands. Saw the tremor. She didn't lie very well.

You can't keep doing this to me.

She reached out, a woman about to touch a hot stove, and laid her hand on his. It was a soft hand, a dark network of veins and thin, delicate fingers. The nails—painted a light shade of pain. Shaped and pointed. Diamond rings on two fingers. The platinum watch banding her wrist a single, shiny manacle.

Her hand was a hand, unlike any hand that had touched him in years. He didn't want it to go away, but he was afraid of its poison and the power it held to make the dream in his groin tear holes in his Levi's. He didn't have to work hard to conjure her up naked. Years of practice with other women had made it easy.

You disappear on me.

I didn't disappear.

Find another place to shop for Dunhills?

Okay. I am chasing you.

What the hell for?

You're someone I can talk to, not many people I can talk to.

Your friend with the ptomaine hair?

A friend, a friend is all.

We don't have anything to say that we haven't already said.

This is private . . .

How private?

All I want is to talk to you . . .

You can't undo time, Karizma. Life's not a song you pick up at the chorus.

Why not?

There's too much blood on the road.

He had trouble speaking through the knot in his brain. More than anything, he wanted to feel her skin, to find out what could have been fifteen years ago.

Can't two people get together and talk about old times without making it a federal case?

I don't want to talk about old times.

He shut off the tirade and the floodtide of desire ebbed. Sometimes you had to Humpty-Dumpty the yolk back in the shell and seal the cracks with pain. He stayed leery of her intrusion into his emptiness. Once you've been empty, you never taste the same. You give up the illusions that make you human and when you look into the dark pit of nothing, nothing is all you see. He didn't remember the day or the hour when he carved despair out of the word hope but he knew he had been soused.

Why are you being so difficult?

How'd you know I was here?

If you want to see a person, you can find that person.

You talked to Casey?

I went by the store, I asked about you. The clerk told me about the trouble you had. You don't have a phone, so I went to your place.

How did you know about my place? The landlady doesn't . . .

Mrs. Miller really likes you.

Mrs. Miller doesn't know me.

She thinks you drink too much.

Karizma lit another Dunhill. The one she'd been smoking still smoldered in the ashtray. Zene studied her in the mirror behind the bar—studied her cheekbones, studied the hair, studied the thick lips that had kiss me painted on them in red.

Her hand lay listless on the bar. A dead fish, a broken butter-fly, a wounded rabbit.

I guess I was wrong . . .

Jesus, Karizma, fifteen years . . . You're married . . .

You can call it that.

Why are you here?

Why do you think I'm here?

What are you offering?

What do you think?

I don't know.

In the mirror, a glaze over her eyes was damming up a river of tears. She stubbed out the first Dunhill and took a long drag on the second.

He looked at the spot where her fingers had lain and his skin was glowing.

You don't have to like me, Zene, just don't hate me.

Zene tried to figure out the genealogy of the wood of the bar while Cyndi changed CDs and Memphis Slim launched into a heavy boogie.

Can we go someplace for a real drink?

I've got to see a man about a horse first.

Zene trucked off to the head. Breathing hard, he stared at himself in the mirror. It used to be easy. Booze. Work. Booze. Sleep. Booze. Women. Booze. Work. She unsimpled it. He didn't like unsimple.

She was standing on the sidewalk, her back to the plate glass window. Her hair glistened in the light, shooting off black flares from the corona of a black sun. In the neon, she glowed with the intensity a red light splashes over dark skin. He knew she was disaster, he also knew she was the most desirable woman he had ever known.

She faced him as he came out onto the street—lust and desire—lips, thick and beautiful with that brilliant red turning black. She was one degree from melting. She walked ahead of him to her car. A big Merc. A big Merc all black and hearse-like and shiny. A Merc that smelled of perfume and cigarettes and the subtle, blood odor of woman.

She handled the car like she belonged in it. He envied her vehicular familiarity. Women who drove expensive cars had to be good drivers.

Down Roosevelt Way through the Roosevelt District to a bar named Dante's near the university where the music was low and the lights, red and lower, and you had to know who brought you, because you couldn't see faces in the gloom.

Dante's

Liquor glasses sweated on little, white, Aunt Gertrude doilies.

Cigarettes stubbed out.

Peanuts in bowls.

When I saw you that first night and you acted like you didn't know me, I was scared to come back.

I don't bite. I don't even bark anymore.

I honestly didn't think I'd ever see you again. The way you just disappeared one day.

I disappeared?

I thought maybe something had happened to you . . . I'm sure your life has been more interesting than mine.

Karizma, just come right out and ask me how in hell I wound up punching cash register keys.

When I walked in there, honestly, I just about fainted . . .

He peered into his glass, a blind man searching for the secrets of the universe, but the bottom of a cocktail glass tells only one story. Double. No chaser.

Okay. The *Reader's Digest* version is that I go to U-Dub get a degree in international relations. I run Jane Hooker's first campaign, she gets elected, I'm her C of S on city council.

Everybody knew you were the only one in our class who was ever going to be important.

Zene put the squeeze on his bourbon to keep it from escaping, and then he glanced up at her. In the red light, her buzz cut was a greyish, reddening halo.

I thought you'd be a senator or something . . .

I lasted through Jane's first term and a piece of the second, but I worked a guy over, so Jane fired me. She made it clear there was no place for a man with my violent nature in public service.

Jane Hooker fired you after everything you did for her?

Yep. Jane rolled out a great big, black ball with my name on it, so I jumped a ferry to Anchorage and put in a year on a crab boat.

Zene pondered the mystery of his drink, but it remained as enigmatic as a verse from Nostradamus. He was still grokking it when the bartender wiped at the bar with a towel and raised his eyebrows.

Zene glanced up, surprised to find himself in a place with humans, none of them masked and all sitting tight together breathing the same air, living on the same edge, death just a cough away. He shoved the empty with his index finger.

And the woman? Zene looked at her the way a hungry man looks at raw meat. Who was she? The virus had taken most of his brain. He didn't taste or smell anything. Who was she and what was she doing beside him on a barstool in Dante's?

You came back to Seattle.

Karizma.

She moved her lips.

He knew who she was but he didn't want to talk any more.

What?

When did you come back to Seattle?

Spent some time drinking and fighting in Mexico, then Yakima, working the fruit. I drove trucks, but there was some trouble. There's always trouble.

Did you ever kill anybody?

Why?

I just wondered.

Do I look like a killer?

So you came back to Seattle.

Landed back in Seattle and drove a bus for a couple of years. I picked night work. Decent people don't ride the bus at night. I figured that if I stayed away from decent people, I'd go deep cover for the rest of my life. Captain of Circles going around the loop of life, picking up scum, and dropping it off. I worked the danger runs in the system looking for trouble.

You drove at night?

I drove at night because there were night rules and you read people to see how dangerous they are and if they say boo, you either boot them off six miles from nowhere or you stomp on them till they're second cousins to flounder.

You make it sound so violent, driving a bus.

She couldn't fathom the idea of a man pounding on the animals until they crawled whimpering back into their cages. How do you tell a normal human being that things change when the animals come out like someone had opened a sewer line to spew slime out on the street?

It is violent. Ninety percent of the people who ride the seven o'clock express downtown won't understand a word out there after ten o'clock at night.

You like it, don't you? Hurting people?

You see hurt people out there. Outlaws and drugs, blood and sex. If it happens after ten o'clock, it's illegal and yeah, I kinda like putting the screws to the loudmouths.

Zene fingered the moisture off the outside of his glass.

Karizma asked how he wound up at 24/7.

Zene told her.

She sipped her drink and there it was, that gesture with the back of her hand wiping away hair no longer there. Zene felt a dose of lust and guilt break out in him.

I don't get this. Fifteen years ago, you stand me and my acne-powered, teenage hormones up . . .

I didn't stand you up on purpose.

The pain in her voice made him look at her again, and when he did, he saw her eyes sparkling like she was sorry for living. Why waste time on her? He had spent chunks of time with curious, ugly, drunk women explaining what his muscles were for, but they were interested in only one muscle and they wanted to know what he was going to do with it and when he was going to do it, and the sooner the better.

He got to his feet.

She had pulverized him just like she had fifteen years ago.

Don't go.

What do you want?

She sloshed the drink around in her glass. The ice tinkled and rattled and danced to an abrupt silence as the music hung up between songs and no one was talking. It was one of those moments with a life all its own waiting for something to happen.

I'm in too deep.

You still got all your teeth.

She laughed, and it was springtime and innocence and purity, and Zene melted—a sugar cube in warm water.

Do you like my mouth?

You have a nice mouth.

Alfred says I have a great mouth.

It's a beautiful mouth, but I don't know how to talk to a woman about her body.

You tell her she's special.

I've only been with ruined women.

How do you know I'm not ruined?

Ruined women can't smile.

Connection

Words disconnected from their meanings built webs and nets of silence. Zene had felt that sensation so many times sitting on a barstool with a woman beside him. They could be talking about the weather, but the feeling that came with it was knowing that you're going to go someplace and fall down together, grasping at each other in a hazy nakedness. Sometimes, it was standing up against a wall in an alley or pawing naked legs in a taxi headed too slow to a hotel or in a car on the street with the windows steaming up or in a hotel on a bed, but the feeling was always the same—first the empty pit in the gut and then the minor tremor in the voice, followed by the sensation of the world centering all its fire and brimstone in the square foot of biomass between the navel and the knees. Procreational ESP, a gonadal language connecting organ to organ. All that remained to determine was when and where and how long.

Zene knew Karizma Carlson wanted to connect. That was fine with him. He had run into a woman once, a Berkeley grad in physical sciences, daughter of money, and a guardian of time who told him there were times when all a lady needs is a good fuck. Zene gave her the verb but didn't ask about the modifier. He left her singing. He never saw her again.

Karizma had matured in fifteen years. The curves were there. The cute girl had become a curious woman. Lines in the flesh around the eyes said hard life. She wasn't a wreck, but in careless moments, her mouth dipped down at the corners—sadness squeezing through the pain and hurt chaining her to hopelessness.

Zene had nothing to lose. He saw anguish flaming like the big, long, red flares they set out around accidents on the freeway when there was blood and broken bone. He'd seen it before, the need that screamed sex when what the woman wanted was to be held and kissed and told she was beautiful and tender and had nice teeth.

Zene hesitated. Karizma laid her hand on his arm, nailing it in place. She was as lost as he was. She was hitting bottom, a buzz-cut mystery wrapped in silk with nowhere to go but down.

The hand morphed into a snake coiling itself around him, venom oozing from its fangs. He didn't pull away.

He fell into the hole between desire and death.

Fifteen years was a long time to wait for a dance.

Kermit the Frog

I'm staying late tonight.

Alfred was standing behind Monica Duncan's desk. Monica had been writing checks to pay bills. She turned in her chair and smiled up at him and asked if he would need her. She bit the eraser of her pen.

I don't think so. Mrs. Gwynn is coming at seven. I'll be setting her temporary and doing the crown work in the lab.

Von Stebbin returned to the dental chair where a five-year-old girl with pigtails held her mother's hand.

Well, sweetie, is your lip numb?

The little girl teared up. Von Stebbin turned to a cabinet behind him. From a drawer, he took out a rubber mask of Kermit the Frog. He slipped it on and turned back to the little girl.

Hi, I'm Kermit.

The little girl laughed.

You don't mind if I look at your teeth do you?

The little girl opened her mouth, the tears drying. Stebbins picked up the drill.

Let's see, maybe if we try this . . .

Half an hour later, the little girl walked out the door with sparkling eyes and an admiring look back at Kermit the Frog.

The Sun Room

Home was a mansion on a hill in Roanoke Park. To the west, the Olympics. To the east, the Cascades, Lake Washington. The perfect location except for the freeway. No matter where you were, Americans going about the business of burning a billion barrels of Arab oil was a background noise. Ambient noise, they called it. The blurry, white noise of civilization as it drives itself into oblivion.

The house, like everything in the country, was worn out. It needed a coat of paint to salve the wounds of time. The lilacs hadn't been pruned. An andromeda in the front yard raged out of control. Brick-bordered flower beds, cracked, broken, circled the house. A professional gardener would have torn it out, built it new from the ground up. The flower beds were not planted to last. Nothing was built to last. Seattle was a microcosm of America—nothing lasts. Nothing is permanent. Nothing.

From the street, a stairway cut between concrete walls to the front entrance and its dismal black door.

Karizma parked the car in the garage under the house.

From the garage, she led Zene up a flight of stairs to a stagnant kitchen in aging blue-and-white tile. The floor was hundreds of octagonal tiles. A wide, yellow border where once money oozed out of the spigots, but it never bought new appliances—visceral patricianism tarnished with worn-out dollar signs.

You married rich.

Alfred's father got into Amazon and Microsoft early and kept buying.

So, you are rich.

He was rich, the father, and he was frugal, meaning he hated to spend money—a defect passed on to the son. He knew electronics were changing the world, so the money kept piling up and every time Microsoft split, he bought more.

How much more?

Alfred doesn't talk about money. It's how he gets even.

Gets even, for what?

For the misery I cause him.

For bringing men home?

I don't bring them home.

I'm the only guy who's ever stood here?

Don't be cruel, Zene.

Don't treat me like an idiot.

You don't know me.

Yeah, right . . .

It's true.

She stood with her back against the door jamb. Her red dress draped over her thighs, blood. She smelled like the latest brand of springtime with a splash of cigarette smoke, a hint of brandy, and the animal scent of runaway estrus. Her skin had taken on the tone some women get in low light—a misty shade of desire.

Zene reached for her. Pulled her to him, brushed her lips but held back, even though the fruit hung low and there was no barbed wire.

She was fire and he knew it.

He walked the road of thorns where every sin ever dreamed led right to the square inch of paradise. He was a man about to suck fire through a straw. He saw the plague, he saw death, he saw transfiguration, every apocalyptic sign ever drawn, ever imagined in the thicket of lust and thorns.

She was death in slow motion exuding the scent of tragedy. Her lips smelled—organic—peach, just at the edge of decay. The voice in his head pounded a song he knew too well—Walk out right now, walk away. Go hide your shame in a bottle of scotch.

That mouth. The mouth, sweet and red, the mouth that caged the warm snake tongue that severed his body from his mind.

Hand on his chest, she peeled loose.

Let me show you the sunroom.

He followed the wake of the sway of her hips up a flight of stairs, up a second set to the top floor to a penthouse with a spa and habitat.

Black fixtures.

Pots with dead plants.

Enormous pots of ficus, philodendron, Norwalk pine.

All dead.

The spa had the feel of a decaying Roman ruin.

He built this for his mother. She died. The futon is for sunning.

Zene pulled her down on the futon.

I can't make love to you, Zene.

His hands slid under her skirt.

Please.

He stopped. Maybe because her scent hadn't killed the last shred of decency left in him. Maybe because she was no longer the girl with cornrows who had set him on fire fifteen years ago. Maybe he was getting old and did not want to fight for something that came so easy.

He backed away.

Adrenalin still shaking him.

She let out a long, jagged breath.

Thank you. I led you on and then turned you off like a prick teaser.

Do they say that anymore?

It's not how I wanted it to be.

When is it ever the way we want it to be?

She smoothed her skirt. Quiet. Looking away.

I was wrong about you, Zene. I thought I saw evil rising in your eyes. If you were rotten, you'd have raped me. It would have been messy, messy, messy.

Couldn't you just tell me you are bleeding?

Would you have come with me if I had?

Yes.

I don't want to say no to you, but it's painful that way.

She crawled on her hands and knees to a low table. He watched the backs of her thighs where on the skin, welts squirmed, red and edgy and brutal. Holding a cigarette box, she crawled to the futon. Sitting on the floor, she lit a cigarette.

Some women can do it, but I can't. A friend of mine . . .

Your friend with the fuchsia do?

She says that if she orgasms during her period, there's not as much pain. If you had me right now, pain is all it ever would be.

That's all it ever is.

The image of her welts hung in his mind, pictures of bruised and scarred fruit cut late from the tree. He had tasted her. He wanted to taste more of her, he wanted to carry her smell on him. But the welts.

There's only one way a woman gets welts like that.

You don't believe that, not one word of it. When I touched you at the bar, you were trembling.

They shared the cigarette, Zene on the futon, Karizma on the floor.

Before this goes any further, you've got to know about me.

I only need to know one thing.

Alfred is older than I am. I want you to know fifteen years of who I am because I'm nothing unless you know everything about me.

I don't need to know anything.

I have to explain why I didn't go with you that night. I have to explain how fifteen years have evaporated and why I'm the way I am.

The welts.

Just listen to me.

Zene wanted to ignore the primitive sadness in her voice, but the pain had eaten into her deep, as deep as she had eaten her way inside him where she was making herself a home in his hollowness. It felt good to have her there, carrying her like he was pregnant with desire.

Loneliness was like that. It turned you off or it attached itself to you the way the virus takes over your DNA until it is part of you and you help it along by living, trying to make it better, finding ways to pass it on, but you knew all the time there were two results—either it went into remission and you lived your life the way you wanted to, or it went out of control and you died.

Zene didn't know which way it was going to be.

He didn't care.

What about the welts?

Karizma, in a cloud of smoke, looked divine, an oracle in the mist of eternity, the smoke coiled over her.

There are men who need to humiliate black women.

Is it worth it?

Everything is your fault.

My fault?

You. Men. Your fault. Everything used to be simple. There were dreams. I hate being grown up, Zene. I hate it.

The void ate the air around them, and in the mist, they were creatures from another time, while outside, the world, everyone continued to move to the tempo and rhythm of living death.

The room.

The room was full of things.

The room in the house was full of objects.

Objects were encyclopedias of experience and hate and disgust, but just then, the void swallowing them was total as the blackest night in a frenzy dream.

Karizma spoke, her voice slipping into the stillness, smooth as a chamois running over slick enamel.

I'm so vulnerable, Zene. Like I'm nobody and I don't belong anywhere.

The confession rode a ripple on her voice, a depressed, somber crease in time that only truth can seal. Truth is indifferent to its own belief. It stands out and can't be taken back.

What do you want, Karizma?

I didn't know my mother. After I dropped out of high school, nothing was easy. Every time I'd go out with a guy, my dad slapped me around because I was his only link to her . . .

The night of the prom, I was trying on the dress and he told me I looked cheap. But that didn't stop him from doing what he always did, and when he finished, I had a black eye and a split lip. I left home and never went back. I don't know if he's dead or alive, and I don't care. The first man who had me was my dad.

The smoke thickened. Thick and ugly and full of truth. Zene wanted to touch her, but the space between them was infinite and as empty as it was ugly.

You don't have anything to say?

When did you cut your hair?

Zene. Please.

You never see your dad?

After what he did to me?

All the time? All the time in high school?

I hated him every time. I was a woman a long time before you asked me out.

And Alfred?

I finished at North Seattle . . .

North Seattle?

Bookkeeping. I got a job as a bookkeeper-slash-receptionist with Alfred. I married him because I didn't have anything better to do and nobody else wanted me.

And the welts?

I told you.

Alfred?

No. But when he touches me now, it's like a slug crawling on me. Once we were at a party and all these successful people were into cocaine and high on all kinds of things, and you didn't know what was going on. I was so young, really, and they were all so chic and sophisticated and I was the mysterious little girl married to the dentist. This guy kept asking me did I want to go to bed with him because he'd never fucked a black woman. Later, men I didn't know would call me up and say they had been at the party, would I go to lunch.

Did you go?

Never.

The welts?

We sleep in different rooms. And now it's like I'm in prison. Every day it gets worse. He's getting more controlling and the only way I can escape is with Charmaine.

Your friend with the ruined face and the fuchsia hair who comes into the shop with you?

Karizma got off the floor. She straddled Zene.

Do you want to use my mouth, Zene?

He did not ask about the welts again.

Karizma drove Zene back to Maple Leaf.

Dropped him on Roosevelt a block from his place.

I don't think we should be seen together.

Okay.

But I want to see you.

Okay. It's your game, you call the plays.

Tomorrow. I'll pick you up at 80th and Roosevelt.

What time?

You get off at midnight.

Zene didn't touch her when she said goodbye.

Karizma

Zene was her chance to rearrange the years so they fit the way she wanted them to.

She was cold and hot at the same time.

Her father no longer owned her. Alfred no longer owned her.

She parked the car in the garage and sat with the motor running.

The welts.

She squirmed. She took a deep breath. She lowered her forehead onto the steering wheel.

If she told Zene the truth about the welts . . .

She would have to tell him about the welts.

Monica

She straddled him in the chair, her dress bunched up around her waist, buttons undone, breasts spilling out of the tight material. She held his head and stroked him and kissed him, cooing an evil smoothness.

You are a worthless worm, Alfred, because you cheat on your wife. Just because it's me you're cheating with doesn't make you any less of a worm.

She doesn't love me.

But you're still in love with her.

No.

You're a liar. And a worm. You're using me to get even with her.

No, that's not true now.

But it was when we started?

Yes, but not anymore.

You love me?

Yes.

Do you see the problem, Alfred? Once you learn to cheat, there's no stopping. You'll find someone else and then you'll cheat on me.

I'd never been with a woman before I married her. You've taught me everything.

Do you know what I feel making love to you? Jealous. You're thinking of her, aren't you? You're still in love with her.

No, Monica. No.

I think you like it when she mistreats you, but then you come crawling to me because you can't ask her to do what you want. You see, sweetheart? She's the real woman because she controls you.

She's a child.

A child who doesn't love you, who doesn't care enough about you to hide her lovers from you.

She doesn't have lovers.

You're a liar, Alfred. Contempt. That's what she has for you. You're using me because she won't have anything to do with you. You are a worm. You'd leave me without thinking about it. Do you like my breasts, Alfred?

Yes.

You can't suck my breasts anymore.

Don't say that.

Would you kill me if I threatened to leave you?

She stroked his cheek with the back of her hand, and let her fingers run to the nipple of his right breast. She pinched it between the fingernails of her thumb and index finger.

Do you like it when I hurt you?

He nodded.

I can't hear you when you shake your head, honey.

Yes.

Tell me what you want me to do.

I want you to do that . . .

No. Tell me exactly what you want me to do to you, Alfred.

I want you to hurt me.

How do you want me to hurt you?

He closed his eyes.

You have to look at people when you ask them to do you favors, honey. If you're looking at your shoes, people will think you're talking to your shoes.

I want you to make me bleed.

She leaned over him and bit him until blood streamed down his chest, bit until he came.

Roosevelt and Eightieth

She was waiting in the parking lot of the surplus store at the corner of 80th and Roosevelt when he got off the bus. She drove south on Roosevelt.

He ran his hand up her thigh. She opened her legs, then closed over his hand and held it in place.

Do you know we wouldn't be here if the Aztecs had invented gunpowder?

Yellow

She came out of the bathroom. She stood in front of him.

Do I look okay in bright yellow?

Your skin was made for bright yellow.

Yellow makes our skin shine.

You wore yellow for me?

Everybody has a color. I think your color is biracial cream.

Did you ever wonder why your navel isn't between your eyes?

What?

It's amazing that our cells all start out the same and then differentiate.

Are you serious? Five minutes ago, you were tongue-tied.

Think how convenient it would be if you had your mouth closer to your stomach, that way you could just shove the food in and not have to chew.

Zene. Look at me.

Why do you have two nostrils but only one mouth? Your best assets are a violation of the rules of nature. But why just one mouth? Why not a backup system? We'd be better off with two. And your trachea is in front of your esophagus. With two mouths, you could have one for talking and one for eating, and you could nosh and rap at the same time. Think about your nose again. Why do you have two nostrils?

She knelt on the bed.

Two nostrils, but only one vagina and swollen labia from too much licking.

Licking is a primal instinct. Yes. Primal.

A Different Woman

She wore a long coat, buttoned high at the neck. Chic sunglasses that hid her eyes. Each time Zene saw her, she was a different woman. Different coats, different skirts, newer shoes. The welts didn't change.

Zene had settled into that helpless zone where life zips by without saying hello and you wind up years older than you should be in human time, the time you wasted stacked up behind you taller than the mountain of future waiting, and you are afraid that your past will catch up with you and she will tell you the truth in a long sentence that always begins with because . . .

At the light at 45th and Roosevelt, she unbuttoned the coat, pulling it away and down over her shoulders.

A pair of cobalt blue shorts and a cobalt blue top covered most of her.

That's not yellow.

Don't you like blue?

Water

They didn't go to the house in Roanoke Park. Instead, she drove down Eastlake and parked on Fairview Avenue by the water.

Zene followed her to a houseboat. No lights.

Inside. She shed the coat. Unsnapped the cobalt blue top.

Zene kissed her. She drew back.

A small table with two place settings in the middle of the room. Wineglasses. Candles. Little white dishes with nuts.

He watched her cook lunch—peppered flank steak, a microwaved yellow Finn potato, a green salad. A healthful meal.

She made coffee, then shed the shorts.

The welts on the backs of her legs raised like fresh, knife-blade scars. Zene didn't like the scars, didn't like what they meant, didn't like what they had cost her. He ran a finger over a welt. She shuddered. He knelt. He kissed the backs of her thighs, licked the welts as if he could lick them off, make them disappear.

Zene, please.

They spent the next two hours trying to figure out how to put the shorts back on.

By two-thirty, she had done everything a woman had ever done to him and he was at work on his third try at teaching her the essence of orgasmic silence.

What do you say to a lady when she vocalizes ecstasy in C-sharp minor?

By three o'clock, the coffee was cold. Above the bed, a skylight filtered Seattle winter-grey light over her. A slip of sweat on her upper lip.

Did you know how to do that in high school?

No, it's a trick a woman taught me in Ecuador.

What was her name?

I don't remember.

She dressed.

Zene watched the welts disappear.

Sliding the coat on, sunglasses, she became a mystery.

¿Y ahora? Que?

Karizma could not look at any part of her body without remembering how his fingers graced it. Until he touched her, she did not exist.

Her breasts were no longer hers as his nails raked the skin. They were two pleasures that his mouth excited and which her fingers fled over at times and dwelt upon at others in a timeless cycle of blind pain and hopeless joy. He guided her through stages of lust and gratification she had not known before. He coaxed her out of her rigid cocoon and lifted her free until she . . . screamed . . . in silence.

They lingered between the ache of seduction and the limbo of desire.

His hands on her thighs closed her eyes as her fire spread.

What she once had taken to be her private thoughts, he squeezed out of her mouth, releasing a debilitating surrender and the fearful exhilaration of embarrassing dampness.

A never-ending flow, her river.

Naked, restless, anxious at the end of their third day on the water.

What do we do now?

What do you mean?

What happens now?

What do you want to happen now?

We can't go on forever like this.

We do what we do, and then we don't do it anymore.

I need to be free.

I don't hold you in.

Does it bother you that I see other men?

Do you?

Would it bother you?

Are you?

I'm a woman. Mysterious women are objects to these men.

I don't own you.

You're not jealous?

I'm not jealous.

Not even a little?

Not even a little bit.

You don't care about me.

We've never kissed with our foul morning breath. I've never smelled you when you stink like a work animal. I've never touched you when you were filthy and sweating. I've never licked you when you were bleeding . . .

When you use my mouth, my breath stinks.

I've never heard you pee . . .

Do you want to hear me pee?

I want to know you as deep as it's possible to know another human being.

Am I human, Zene? I don't think I'm human anymore.

Kneeling at her feet, Zene stroked her thighs with his nails and the small death swept over her—so fast—then vanished and life became dangerous and Zene knew what she was asking of him.

Her Mouth

She winced.

What's the matter.

Nothing.

He folded his napkin on the table and braced his hands under his chin. He looked at her for several minutes until she glanced up.

It's that second molar, isn't it?

No, I'm all right.

I told you we'd have to keep a watch on it. Come down to the office and let me look at it.

No. It's nothing.

Karizma, I saw pain just now.

It's nothing, Alfred.

If you're in pain when you chew, the nerve is already affected. If you let it go too long, it'll become necrotic and you'll need the root canal you probably already do.

Why do you get that prissy sound in your voice when you talk to me?

It's my job to give people the best care that I can.

She tossed her napkin on the table and left the room. Alfred ate in silence. The clicking of silverware on china had a monastic, bell-like quality.

He looked at the plate with the remains of the meat loaf on it. Meat loaf and green peas with sliced almonds again. Canned fruit cocktail in a dessert cup and three French rolls that Karizma had bought from La Française, a bakery in Wallingford where people in Volvos spent Saturday morning drinking coffee and munching on croissants. He had told her not to shop there again, but she had. He was going to punish her for it.

He wiped his mouth with the napkin and folded it beside his plate.

He walked to the bottom of the stairs and looked up. He heard her moving around in her room.

Karizma?

The mouse-like noises stopped. She stood at the top of the stairs looking down at him.

I won't go with you. I'll get somebody else to look at it . . .

How are you going to pay for it?

I'll find a way.

Crowns and root canals are expensive, but when you need an implant . . . Do you have enough money to handle an implant?

You could give me the money.

I could give you the money, of course I could, but then you'd go to one of my colleagues and what would he think?

Professional courtesy, that's what he'd think, Alfred. There are some specialists in this world. You're not an endodontist. Other human beings do have skills.

Of course they do, but you're not married to them, Karizma. You know what's in store if you don't let me do it. First, the nerve dies, then it will decay and the gas will build up inside the pocket, and the pain will be unbearable for a short time . . .

I can't hear you, Alfred.

She leaned over the banister, glaring at him.

. . . and if you don't attend to it, the decay will eventually go into the bone. That's when the real pain starts . . .

Give me the money.

Oh, I'll give you the money when you are ready to pay the interest.

She slammed the door.

He went into the kitchen for a glass of water. He set the glass on the tiled counter and stood for a few seconds looking at the sink. Then he went down to the garage.

Mrs. Childress's Mouth

At his office, Alfred turned on the lights in the lab and picked up the phone. Karizma answered.

Karizma, the longer you wait, the worse it will get.

The line went dead. He called again. She did not answer.

He picked up the mold of the full set of teeth.

He held a sculpted tooth. A peg emerged from the center. He set the crown with a mixture of porcelain and gold. The yellow cast of the metal fused with the ivory-tinted porcelain. It was a masterpiece, a miniature sculpture that represented the state of the art in metallurgy and enamels. A finer craftsman would not find any flaw in it.

With ease, he set the crown onto the peg and held the model up to the light. He examined it then, pressing it into place, he took the pick and felt the margins. When it was set in place, the crown would meld with the remainder of the actual tooth into a perfect bond that would last for twenty or thirty years.

Such a shame. Such a work of art hidden inside Mrs. Childress' mouth.

Pain

I have to set Mrs. Gwynn's temporary cap, and I have some other prep work to do. I can see you after Mrs. Gwynn.

What time?

She's coming at seven, takes me an hour because she wants nitrous oxide . . .

To set a temporary?

People are strange when it comes to the dental chair.

Alfred watched her spoon a serving of tuna casserole and chew it on the right side of her mouth. He smiled when she winced. She did not look at him.

The Patient List

Alfred did his own lab work for less than many dentists, and he took evening patients. He was a good dentist. He had the soft touch. His apparent senescence—the grey hair, the creased skin—inspired a sense of grandfatherliness. He could be the man who used to appear in ads about dentists, and toothpaste and floss. Avuncular with a speculum reflector on his forehead and a smile on his lips. Alfred Von Stebbin was the archetypal dentist.

His clients knew he wasn't golfing in Hawaii on their crowns.

The Cost Plus Interest

Karizma settled in the chair. The equipment in the office was not new. The chair was the heavy kind, more barbershoppish than dentish. The light was huge and covered with a chromium sheath in a look once popular in science fiction movies about mad dentists who created monsters.

And all the equipment was in shades of lime green, including the lab coat Alfred wore. The office smelled the way a dentist's office should smell—Lavoris mouthwash with a sub-layer of cinnamon. It had the hush of quiet expectation. The only sounds were the hiss of the air from the compressor and the gurgle of water in the spittoon beside the chair.

Alfred waited until Karizma was settled, then he alligator-clipped the bib on her and smoothed it over her chest. She was shaking. He smiled.

He pressed the foot controls of the chair. Karizma reclined. When she was supine, Alfred touched her face.

He was a professional. She didn't flinch when the dentist touched her, but when he felt her body as her husband, she was sickened and her skin crawled.

Alfred's fingers explored her mouth. The clicking of instruments against the enamel of her teeth. The scent of cinnamon.

A gentle touch. His injection technique without trauma. She opened her eyes to look at the ceiling where Alfred had pasted a copy of an Escher intaglio print, *Relativity*.

He turned the probe and tapped her teeth.

Feel anything?

Uhh.

Alfred worked a pathway from the buccal to the lingual side.

I'm going to take a picture of that bad molar.

He placed the film in her mouth. He positioned the x-ray machine, then ducked out of the room, came back, and lifted the film from her mouth.

I'll deaden you while that develops.

He reached to the instrument tray and came up with the syringe.

You'll feel just a little pinch.

The needle penetrated her gum.

He left her in the chair, the taste of clove in her mouth.

He returned holding the x-ray in a clip.

It's deep, Karizma. Bad.

He pushed away from her on the rolling chair.

She lay in the chair in a dreamy state.

She saw him backlit in a halo of brightness as he blocked the light and peered down at her.

The gas mask.

She tried to pull away.

He pressed the mask tight over her face.

She gasped. She wanted to hold her breath.

He pushed her back into the chair.

And Later

When she woke, it was daylight and she was swinging in a sea of nausea and she ached and as she raised her hand to her eyes, the pain in her arm was a sharp, deep jabbing.

She looked at the clock. Eight o'clock. She was in her own bed. Alfred?

Her voice echoed hollow, cold, distant. She was alone.

She sat up. Her head throbbed. She swung her legs over the edge of the bed. She was sore. Legs, buttocks, thighs.

She was naked. Alfred had brought her home. He had undressed her.

She staggered to the bathroom and sat on the toilet.

She ran her fingers between her legs and smelled his odor.

She gagged.

She remembered nothing.

Rising, she looked at herself in the mirror. She looked ill. She swayed, dizzy and short of breath.

She splashed water on her face, then stepped into the shower. She scrubbed between her legs, scrubbing as if water could undo what he had done to her. She was bruised. Her bottom ached. He had taken her there.

On her left arm, a bruise. She poked at the yellow-and-blue flesh, an abstract work of art in its mix of colors. Her right arm ached. Her cheeks hurt from the mask. Red splotches on her thighs. She sobbed as she scrubbed at her bottom.

Out of the shower, she looked at her body in the mirror—belly reddened. Thighs rough. Vagina sore. She closed her eyes. What had he done to her this time?

She pulled on a pair of patterned hose. No garter. The pain. She closed her thighs. Pain ripped into her stomach. Nausea.

She dressed in a black woolen skirt and a white woolen sweater with a loose cowl neck. She slipped on a pair of black flats.

Her hips ached. Her feet felt inflamed. Her buttocks. Oh.

She went downstairs. Each step a jab at her breasts.

The house was pregnant with pain. She wanted coffee. The clinking of the spoon against the side of the cup made her nervous. Images flashed through her mind—the mask, the injection. The eyes. His eyes. She stood looking at the black liquid in the cup. Nausea. This time, he had been different.

This time, he had tried to kill her. If he killed her who would know? There was no one to worry about her. The emptiness around her expanded.

Dizzy. Hollow dizziness.

No breath. A vicious swirling caught her up and she fell and the tile of the kitchen floor slammed against her cheek and there was darkness.

Twenty-Four Seven

The phone ringing hung in her mind like a huge fingerprint on a sea of blackness. She opened her eyes. The phone kept ringing. Then it went silent.

She lay on the floor, staring at the splash board around the bottom of the kitchen cabinets. The light in the kitchen, grey and meager. The tile cold. Her cheek wet. She had fallen, and in falling, had dropped the cup and spilled the coffee. The smell of coffee made her ill.

She arched her back and tried to stand.

But her body didn't behave.

She knee-walked to the small drawer for the phone book.

She found the 24/7 on Roosevelt Way. She dialed the number, a woman answered. She asked for Zene. He comes in at four. Karizma hung up. She couldn't remember the name of the woman who ran his house.

She was crying. She did not want to cry.

Tears gave way to a crystal-clear vision of a name—Mrs. Miller.

She leafed through the book until she found a Miller on Roosevelt. She dialed. A woman answered.

I need to find Zene.

Zene?

Silence. Then, a voice soothing and warm and rich.

Yeah.

Zene . . .

Karizma?

Can I see you?

I just got up.

Please . . .

Her head ached.

I hate myself, Zene. I have to see you.Okay.

Lake Union

At 80th and Roosevelt, Zene checked his watch. The bus was late. It came crowded with students going to the U and office workers heading downtown.

The houseboats on Lake Union are all moored on the east shore of the lake south of the Ship Canal. The University Bridge carries heavy traffic from the University District along Eastlake Avenue to downtown. Fairview Avenue East is a short street that runs between Lake Union and Eastlake for a few blocks, then dead-ends at the Canal to the north, but connects up farther south to Mercer Street.

The Eastlake houseboat enclave lived loose around the edges and took a lot for granted about human nature. Up the street, there was a little store called Pete's Supermarket. It wasn't a supermarket, and Pete probably didn't own it anymore. But the people on the boats didn't go to Safeway, they went to Pete's. And just up the hill, on Lynn Street, there was the Eastlake Zoo and Fat Albert's, both old-time, hell-raiser taverns where all the young people got together and drank after having dinner at Julia's Fourteen Carrot Cafe, a premiere vegetarian health food café.

Zene remembered the summer day he had walked down the gangway from Minor Street passing a party on one of the houseboats. Bikini-naked women sat in the sun drinking from tall glasses and listening to loud music. They hadn't paid any attention to him because he was the wrong age, height, and build. They were hungry for young meat with deep Porsche potential. He had watched them until they stared at him and giggled in his direction.

This time, it wasn't summer. He got off the bus at Nick and Sully's, which was too far south, and had to walk back.

He saw her car backed into a slot. He opened the door and looked inside. No blood. That was good.

A cold wind blew in off Lake Union. His breath clouded as he walked down the gangway. Across the water, Gas Works Park stood on the north shore of the lake, distant, the skeletal, metallic remains of postindustrial, gutted dreams.

Zene knocked on the door.

No answer. He tried the handle. Unlocked. He walked into a darkened room.

His eyes adjusted to the dull, grey, liquid-like light filtered through thick curtains on an urban disaster—clothing strung around, dirty dishes on the drainboard, records and tapes out of their covers—the background noise to the crumbling of psyche and civilization, the soft thumping of jazz sax coming from the radio. Little red amplifier lights glowed in the dark.

Zene waited, thinking that somewhere a body lay dead and bleeding, but he didn't want to see it, know about it—how do you measure your good against all your mistakes? And he had made a mistake.

Karizma.

He turned to leave, but stopped and peered into the greyness, and there he saw her face—streaked, cold, frightened.

He went to her. She was shaking.

There was a moist and morgue-like smell about her body. He smelled pain. He smelled despair. His nostrils filled with it. He knew the scent of hurt, the aroma of fear.

It was a mistake.

What was a mistake?

I shouldn't have called.

I'm glad you did.

Something really crazy has happened.

She wiped at her eyes. Zene felt the veil of fear, its warp and weft, the ragged hyperventilation of a half-controlled hysteric.

Zene pulled her against him. She was a jungle, damp, but her hair smelled of a spring rain. Fire flared in him. He pushed it down. She was ripe, vulnerable, helpless. Open as a tulip in sunlight and as fragile.

Tell me.

Alfred tried to kill me last night.

Her voice ripe in the matter-of-fact way you describe a dog getting a rabies shot. She sobbed—a half-choked gurgle.

Why?

I've made mistakes.

People make mistakes. They don't get killed for them.

Alfred. He hates every penny I spend. I have no money. He bought me that car, he owns the house, he makes such a big deal out of buying food. He thinks it'd be better if I starved or something. He lets me buy some clothes, but he wants the charge card back after I've been shopping, and I have to show him the slips. I'm a slave. And last night, he tried to kill me.

He tried to kill you because you went shopping?

I haven't been good, Zene.

It came out in short bits and tiny pieces over a long time and it didn't start where he thought it would or end up where it should have.

Four years ago, I met Charmaine.

The broken woman with fuchsia hair.

Yes. I needed money. Charmaine had contacts at Deja Vu, a club on Lake City Way. I didn't think at first I could do it, but I had no choice, he keeps me penniless.

You danced in a club.

Well. More than danced.

And that's why Alfred tried to kill you?

She picked at her fingernails. Zene had mastered the art of silence. He waited with her.

I have to tell you all of it, Zene. I'm not joking when I tell you there've been times when I wondered where my next meal was coming from.

Does he know about the club?

If he does, he'd hate anyone who helped me.

Tell me what he did to you.

She told him about the chair, the injections, the gas, and winding up naked and sick in bed. The telling was cold, leftover sausage, but in her voice, Zene heard the growl of the shadow of death.

This isn't the first time. Two years ago in August, he made me go with him to Moses Lake. Hate going anywhere with him. It didn't seem like much at the time, but he took back roads, and then he stopped the car, because, he said, something was wrong with it. We were down in a gorge, somewhere in eastern Washington. He said he could fix it, but Alfred's not a mechanic and the car wouldn't run after that at all . . .

I was wearing shorts and a halter top and flipflops because I thought we were coming back that night. I didn't have a change and he didn't want to leave me there because it might be a long time before he found a tow truck.

He opened the trunk for a pack. I didn't ask why he had a pack. I knew I shouldn't have gone, but it was go with him or sit there and burn up in the car . . .

But you made it.

He made it. After about an hour, I couldn't go on. Everything looks the same out there, but I was certain we were going in circles. I kept falling behind him, so he sent me back to the car. And he left me out there to die.

But you didn't die.

I found my way to the car, but Zene . . . I was sick and it was dark before he came back and it was like he expected me to be dead. It was like he hadn't been in the sun at all. He got the car started, and he drove to Wenatchee. He took me to a hospital. The doctor said I was lucky to be alive because I had heat prostration and I was dehydrated.

Did you tell this to the police?

What was there to tell?

You thought he wanted you to die. Go to the police now.

I can't.

Why?

I told you, I've made mistakes.

Tell me again.

She took a deep breath and let it out. She picked at her fingernails.

Charmaine and I. There are these stag parties. I only do it because I need the money. Don't hate me, Zene.

If we were perfect, we wouldn't have to try so hard, would we?

But there was more, Zene . . .

Zene waited. She was off somewhere, running a tape in her mind. He saw it in the way her mouth twitched and her eyes fluttered. She made up her mind to tell him what he already knew. The welts, the used-up woman with fuchsia hair, the late night rendezvous. He waited for her to come back.

Some men get off hurting women . . . it's not a simple thing, Zene.

The welts . . .

There's more.

She went away again, and when she came back, her voice broke, and she looked at him through tears.

Do you hate me, Zene?

You're down, Kari. I know all this. I've been down there too.

You called me Kari. That's the name I used. I hadn't been out in the world, Zene. I didn't know men could be so perverted. You read about it, but until you get there, you don't know . . . you know everything now, you control me too . . .

I don't want to control you.

You know a woman's sins, you control her . . .

I knew a woman whose grandmother had survived the camps. She ate garbage, she lied, she cheated. And, if you knew what she was saying, you could see that her body was her currency. How many loaves of bread could a woman get for taking a man in her mouth?

Karizma lit a cigarette, exhaled. The smoke was sweet.

Then I met this attorney. We started seeing each other.

When?

I wasn't made for his kind of love. We had this game. We'd go to bed and while he put ropes on me, I'd call Alfred. And I would be coming and Alfred would be telling me that he had done a root canal that morning.

You don't have to tell me this, Karizma.

I need you to get me out of the mess I'm in.

You're not still seeing the attorney . . .

No, but at the club . . .

Since we've been together?

I need money, Zene. God you can't imagine how I need money.

Walk away from it.

From Alfred?

From everything.

I need someone to make me stop.

I can't help you there.

You have to. You're the only one who can. Once you've been filthy, you have to make yourself clean. But sometimes you need help. When I saw you in the store, I thought there is a way out. You were there, someone who knew me when I was different, just like that, out of the blue, and I knew you would help me.

There's only one way out of this.

You and I can go away together.

No, Karizma. You cut your losses, you leave without me holding your hand.

There's one other way.

Zene heard her say it, and he felt the messy nudge of wickedness press him. She lay back and covered her eyes with her arm.

He knew what she was saying. In the long silence, he felt her, smelled her odor and felt her tension, and the tension tasted like powdered Spanish Fly.

He knew what she wanted. He had to decide.

Does he know about us?

No one knows about us.

Not even Charmaine?

Not even Charmaine.

Alfred knows.

Maybe.

Divorce him.

He's not worth anything to me divorced, but dead, he's worth a lot.

There was the residue of the misty innocence in her eyes, the innocence before her purity died leaving her without scruples or morals or any personality, and stripped her naked as if she had peeled off her human skin down to bone and teeth, and there was nothing to touch but poison and evil and death, and he wanted to kiss her, to take her right then, and she wanted him to.

Then, the look faded and she was nothing. A cold, hard nothing.

That's dangerous talk.

The bruises . . . You don't believe . . .

She drew her legs up under her and wrapped her arms around her knees and rocked back and forth and Zene needed to touch her, needed to feel her evil in the palm of his hand, to rub his hand on her skin and lick her sickness from his hand.

The DJ was running an Ornette Coleman piece. In Coleman there was no music, as if he had found a way to make silence out of noise. The track ended.

He injects me with sodium pentothal and then when I'm un-conscious, he takes me and does things to me.

She took a long breath in several staggered gasps.

Closed her eyes.

A minute. Two.

She opened them and the nothingness had turned to an anger he'd never seen.

One night, we had an argument down in Interlaken Park. We were coming back from a party or something, I don't remember. He started to call me names and said I was ugly and he didn't want to be around me anymore.

When we got home, he told me I was hysterical. That night, he gave me the first injection. I always come out of it sore and bruised, not just on my arms, but every orifice in my body feels like it's been whipped, Zene. Last night was different. I don't know what it was. I don't know what he used. When I woke up, I was messy and bleeding and I knew he expected me to die.

What are you asking me, Karizma?

Kill him for me, Zene.

The cold runs over you when you stand naked in front a hiss-ing snake and you know you've got a couple of seconds before you die, but she said it in plain language, and the way she said it, it didn't sound so bad. Not bad at all.

Fireflies of the Mind

Zene lay on his back looking at the shadows on the ceiling. Zeros. He was tired of reinventing himself. The past sprawled out behind him—broken glass, brittle steel, spikes, and thorns.

And blood. His blood.

Starting over got harder each time. Everything, every time dropped to zero. He had torn off everything a man could call a life—he lived in a single room with no future, a future with no chance. When he got down to it, there was no place to go, nothing to do except mark time.

Mark time.

Then what?

A black hole grew in his mind. Migraine flashes at the corners of his eyes, flecks that bounced and flickered—small brush fires melting his brain.

He rolled onto his side.

Looked out the window.

Grey. Dark. Endless.

He had never wanted to kill a man. It wasn't something you did, like brushing your teeth. What did a dead man get him? Not the woman. Wouldn't get him the woman. Sure of that. What then?

Lucifer rising. Murder taking hold of him. It had been there before, but before he had squeezed it out of his mind—he did know how—close his mind to drive evil back into the dark.

Now it was a choice, an obvious choice. To shake hands with evil had a sweet sense of perversity. But then?

Make that decision and still be human?

The sad part of what he had become was seeing himself say yes to, yes to and even wanting a murderous act in the drama that always before he had pretended not to see it, not to know about it, by letting the violence in him take its head, to work its way into the world though his fists. That was. That was him. But going past that? Into it all the way?

Kill him for me, Zene.

Now he was sure that the part of him hidden in his violence was the core of his character. The violence was his real self. She read that violence, used that skin to unleash it . . .

He rolled onto his back, looking at the shadows on the ceiling, shadows that opened into deep holes ripe with hopelessness.

Kill him for me, Zene.

The veneer that had caused him to close his eyes to it was the thin, half-hearted layer of civilization that separated him from his nature. To be human and to kill was as natural as breathing. Evil lived cloaked in good, permutations of a will to power frustrated by the gentility of civilization. Civilization once locked the chains on evil. Laws punished men who let it out, but Zene, as he lay on the bed in the room in the house on Roosevelt, knew that civilization was losing and there was no redemption, there was only action, and if he won, if his evil triumphed, then it would, as other prince-makers had averred, become good. The katagogic spiral spun down until the only goodness left in the race lay in the moment of conception when pure innocence had not yet been perverted by a single breath.

This theology of dread explained the state of the human in the universe.

Zene glanced at the body on the floor.

A body. His body? Whose body? A body.

The discourse budding in his head grew, each tiny thought budding, growing into larger, cohesive flowers of evil, shattering back into unconnected shards, only to reassemble themselves as other ideas outside his will to control them.

Would she save him?

The one flaw was the ending. He knew the end. It was as inevitable as his death. Did it matter? Yes. It mattered. To die was natural, to hasten his own death was not.

In a dark place in the back of his mind was the solace that the most he'd get would be time in prison. Washington wasn't executing anyone. The prisons were full of men who ought to have been dead, but who continued to live while the executioners tried to find a better way. Some of them wanted to get the method changed to a more pristine way to murder. Murder begetting murder. Death sentences prolonged through a series of endless appeals. Either way, nobody was dying, but everyone was dying and everyone deserved to die, but only the innocent were being annihilated.

Zene had fought the hanging battles because hanging was repugnant to most people, so if they found a way to clean death up, more people would die. More men would die.

Euthanasia for the criminal mind. They weren't having much luck. It made no difference—being in prison or being outside, the results were the same. Walls everywhere.

Holes everywhere.

Nowhere to go but down.

Zene weighed the pros and cons. Holding her, feeling her against him. Tasting her. Was that enough reward for the cost? It was some consolation. But was it enough? Each time he held her and looked at her and worshipped her it would cost him a few years.

He didn't want to love her, but she was a way back. He could undo fifteen years of misery. He could live with her, love her, love her hair, love her mouth and teeth, love her legs and her skin, love all of her—everything he needed to start over was in her. He had only to cross over. Once over, he would be back. He would be dead, but he would be back.

Birthing desire for her was part of her plan. She knew that. She knew what he was. He knew what was going on. He used her for his pleasure, trying to guess what she had in mind as she used him to release her madness, her evil, her own desire to be desired.

Zene rolled onto his back to stare once again at the ceiling, arms behind his head. If it could be done, just how would he do it?

There were always things that went wrong.

Sometime later, he drifted into sleep, and as he did, he felt his erection rising. Death? Love? Sex? A nice, warm, moist feeling—not desire, but desire was the fire that ignited it. Desire for what he did not know. Money? Sex? Her? Death?

His dreams that night were gentle, transient reveries full of flowers and a blue sky. Somewhere. And rolling hills.

Six Hundred Seventy-Eight Dollars and 37 Cents

Alfred Von Stebbin looked up from the display catalogs Jim Thompson had laid out on his desk.

I don't understand.

Al, you and I done more than a bit of business. Okay. Upstairs, they kicked it back to me because I service your account and the amount of the billing was less that what we got paid. They told me to check it out.

I still don't understand, Jim.

He looked at the check, and then at the invoice. The bill was for $768.37, and the check was for $678.37.

It's okay. I mean, they'd have just sent you another bill, but I told them I was coming out so they save a little with the postage.

It's not okay. A hundred dollars here and there and you're talking big money quick.

He took off his glasses, wiped at his eyes, massaged the orbital bones with the palms of his hands. Jim Thompson closed his briefcase.

Here's what I figure. Your clerk just reversed the numbers. Happens a lot. 768, 678. See, just a reversal.

I'll talk to Monica on Monday. She can straighten it out.

When Jim Thompson was gone, Alfred sat at the desk holding the check. The bank hadn't fouled up. The mistake wasn't just a switched number. Something was going on and he didn't know what it was.

At home, Alfred sat through a silent dinner of baked pork chops, green beans, and rice with sliced almonds in it. Karizma's hostility flowed at him in waves from the other end of the table. She hadn't spoken to him since the chair, but he knew that under that quiet shield she was seething. Alfred felt like a man spread-eagled over an earthquake fault, waiting for it to act up and split him in two. She hadn't asked him for money for a week. He didn't understand that.

He went back to the office and sat down at Monica's desk. He pulled the ledger and the checkbook. Alfred wasn't a bookkeeper. He looked at the billings for several patient accounts. Then he studied the invoice from Dental Supply. One by one, he went over the accounts and totaled the entries in the check book.

At three o'clock, he closed the ledger. He thought he knew how it had been done. But he didn't know why. With the cancelled checks, he could be sure. But the bank no longer returned cancelled checks unless you asked for them, and then they would give you a microfiche and not the check itself. He would have to go to the bank in the morning and take a look at those checks.

He sat back in the chair and closed his eyes. When he opened them, there were tears at the corners. He was angry and hurt. The question was the size of the losses. He knew they were enormous.

Monica started to work for him and his expenses had gone way up. It looked so innocent. Inflation? Added expenses? That was some of it. But not all of it. He had to talk to her before he made any decisions.

Alfred went to the files to look for Monica's address. Until then, he hadn't bothered to look it up. There had been no need. Every time he had wanted her, she was there, and when he wanted to go to her place, she refused.

She lived in Crown Hill. He drove out Greenwood to Holman Road, went down to 15th NW. Crown Hill was quiet at three-thirty in the morning.

He sat in the car at the curb looking at the building. It was four floors of white stucco trimmed with hostile shrubbery and darkened walkways. It had been built in a hurry and would rot just as fast, but probably not before the rip-off artist who'd developed it sold it for a profit and had found a beach in Hawaii. That was the way they did it. Either that or a place in the woods on the east side. Sometimes both.

He tried the door of the building. Locked. He looked at the mailboxes. Penciled under her name in faint lettering was another name, Iqbal Mahmoud.

Alfred got back in his car and sat for a while staring straight ahead. It was no longer a mystery. He drove back home, went up to his room, and lay on his bed, staring at the ceiling. Tears rolled down and into his ears.

At dawn, he fell asleep.

The Earthy Scent of Sweat

The car slipped into the garage and the Genie sealed them up. They waited for the timed light on the opener to go out.

In the dark, he smelled her, fresh and clean, the damp scent of the perfume of her cleft untainted by the strong odor of cigarette smoke. Under the perfume, the frail scent of excitement that gave way to the earthy smell of sweat.

This is the most dangerous thing we can possibly do meeting like this, going on like this. Here.

In the dark, her hands found his face. She kissed him.

The first one they suspect when a man dies is his wife.

He was rational. She was fire. Vibrating waves of desire rolled over him, enveloped him in a Morphean aura.

I die every day I don't see you.

Think, Karizma.

I don't want to think.

Her hand groped his crotch, her tongue melted in his ear. He moved his head.

We've got to get some things straight . . .

Fuck me, Zene.

Her voice brushed him, a feather whisking past his ear.

He wanted to pull away from her, but the tongue and the hands nailed him in place. He measured the hurt and the fear and the shame against desire.

Her mouth closed again on his. She pulled his soul out of his body and left a vacuum and he was going to implode. The excitement she exuded was thick as glue. Every time they made love now, it was savage. His brain locked down. They rutted until they were incapable of moving. He couldn't resist that. He wanted to call her names, to defile her and at the same time to deify her.

His hands wormed their way under her skirt. No underwear, thigh-high stockings she now wore each time they met. His fingers dug at her openness. She squirmed to the passenger side of the car and opened her legs. Zene on his knees. In the darkness, her aroma filled his nostrils, rushed into his head.

When he went into her she was gushing hot iron.

She grunted, pushed against him, forcing him deeper into her, her arms not around him but flung out, her teeth grinding until she gasped and hung poised on the crest.

And she came, ramming him in, wildness unhinged and then fallen, she picked herself up again. She had no limits. Zene wanted to be so far in her that he became part of her. If he fused with her, the only way she could destroy him would be to destroy herself. But it wasn't the kind of fusion that ever took place in the flesh, and they melted together and he stayed in her until she made him rise.

This time with her was not like any other time. Impossible intensity. Before, when he felt himself coming alive in her, every time he came in her, it had been as though they had invented intensity. But this, he knew, was eternity. This was the last time. The epiphany. The apotheosis. The ennoblement of desire. The final spasm of existence.

This had never happened before, because as he was making love to her, his mind was split in two, and half of it was thinking about what it meant and when he would die.

Wrapped in her, her sexuality engulfing them, Zene was frightened, because he was a dead man and Alfred was going to die, that was now certain, but he, Zene, was also dead, and so it was one dead man killing another dead man, and where was the morality in that? If the dead killed the dead, who cared?

Karizma's sweat covered him. Moisture in her hair, on her skin. Her lips raked over his face, her hands clawed at him, and each time she collapsed against the car seat as though she had died.

Who would care? Someone might. Fifteen years of forget remembered in the front seat of a car in a dark garage under the house of a dead man.

The police looked at murder by other men, but they themselves were innocent. If you killed a man and got caught, you had to pay.

Karizma, silent now, the rage calmed, the dread overcome, she drew him down into her, her now cool lips gliding over his cheek, petting him as though he were a small animal. And he wallowed in her touch.

Zene knew the price. He was the sacrifice, but that no longer mattered. He had been so deep in Karizma, Karizma, whose heat had not faded from him even after fifteen years, and nothing mattered now.

How could he look at another woman after the complete, savage, and barbaric way they pulled each other to the edge? They were somewhere no one had ever been. Thunder. Transformation. Animals transformed into sexual energy. She would be good to him for a while. But afterward? *Zene, I don't think we should be seen together.* It didn't matter. There would be no afterward. This was the end. The complete and utter finality of existence. A cycle of arousal and consummation so powerful they had become nothuman. He was lost in her as he now knew he would have been had he held her in the dance of death fifteen years before. And nothing mattered. No.

The Bargain

If I do this for you, you own me, forever.

It's a two-way street.

How do you know I won't let you down?

You won't let me down because you love me and there's salvation in love, Zene. Isn't that what they say? If you love someone, they live in you even if you are dead, even if they are nothing.

I don't know what they say. Most of the people I know aren't very articulate about love. Is there a moral question?

You think I have any morals left? I gave up morality the first time my father fucked me, the first time I took my G-string off in a roomful of drunk men, or was it the first time he knocked me out and I didn't leave him?

We have to clear up some things. Like insurance. Is there insurance?

Maybe. I think he told me that he had some ADA stuff, but it's not much and I haven't signed up anything on him.

It's got to be clean.

She looked at him, and then again, like she understood for the first time what was actually going to happen.

Zene . . . How are you going to do it?

What Do You Know About Dying?

It would happen, she would find out about it and be shocked, saddened, surprised. The police would work on her, they always did, and unless she was innocent, they would break her down, break the shock into submission, the sadness into admission, the surprise into punishment. Her ignorance was his only salvation.

She showed him a sheaf of papers she'd taken from Alfred's desk. Zene discovered nothing in them but a policy on Karizma through the professional association. One hundred-thousand-dollar payout for spouses. Alfred had been very careful to keep the information booklet with the policy. It included an AIDS

Policy Statement. Before he could get insurance on himself, he had to submit to an HIV test. There was no evidence that he had. He had carried the policy on Karizma for several years, but eighteen months ago, he hadn't renewed it.

Karizma wasn't covered. It didn't make sense.

That night as he lay in bed, Zene figured out the puzzle.

Everything Karizma told him fit into place.

Alfred wanted her dead.

He had cancelled her policy.

With the policy in force, the insurance company would have been all over him.

Zene's brain crackled. It creaked. It fell apart. Shame spilled out into the slime of degradation and ruin and deceit. But he would do it.

He was caught in spheres of hell that he understood. Wheels would crush his bones, gears grind his bones.

Every minute of every day of every month of every year he had sunk deeper.

Just a few centuries before, he had been a naïve kid duking it out with bullies on the street, but now he was Mr. Sophisticate wrapped up in the killer game with real killers in the warp and weave of death. Killers—the ones who do it and get away with it. And he would do it.

Yesterday, he had known nothing about the universe, but now he was one with every nuance, every crevice, every niche in it, and he knew he was dead.

The stars were no problem.

The galactic glue was no mystery, because he now understood human nature.

Alone in the universe, that was the key. Alone, you are crushable, you are time-prey, you are not even dust.

Karizma was alone.

Alfred wanted her to disappear.

He would kill her.

She would disappear and no one would notice that she was gone.

No one would care. Zene did not want her to stop shining and disappear, forgotten into the comic dust.

He would do it.

Execution

Zene parked on Third Avenue north of 85th Street and walked to the Fred Meyer. He checked his watch, then went into the phone booth where he stood with his finger on the dial and the receiver at his ear. To anyone seeing him, he was talking. The conversation was imaginary. The shrill ring of the phone was not.

He jerked his finger away. A pause. He heard her breathing. He waited for her to speak. Cosmic dust.

Go ahead.

A long emptiness, as though she wanted to say something else, but she hung up. She would hang up and take a heavy sedative. Sleep. No question of where she was. While she slept, Zene would release her from fate, free her from her chains and she would hear about it in the morning.

Zene set the phone into the cradle. He waited fifteen minutes, each minute a slice of eternity on a planet twirling in planetary waste, ruin a few minutes away.

He drew the blackjack from under the car seat.

The blackjack. A simple piece. A sack of black leather filled with ball bearings wrapped with duct tape. One technological step beyond a club. He had made it one afternoon while sitting in his room looking at the Olympic Mountains.

He turned the corner. He walked east on 85th Street. He took a new pair of gloves from his hip pocket and jammed the gloves tight. Good leather gloves, tight, thin, pliant pigskin so soft.

He walked the block-and-a-half to Alfred's office.

He breathed short, strangling, night-time gasps at the entrance to the building on Greenwood Avenue. It was a somber brick structure with a large, modern glass doorway that destroyed the integrity of the early century architecture.

Alfred had the second-floor corner office. The gold lettering on the street-side windows had flaked off, leaving the name in ruin—.LFRE. V.N STEB.IN. DDS

The first key opened the outer door. Zene pulled the key out of the lock and tucked it back into his pocket.

The stairs had a smell simmering between old tar and anesthesia.

No sound other than the muffled tread of a foot on a heavy rubber pad.

A wooden handrail turned on the landing. Zene stood in a long hallway branching left and right and lined with milk glass doors—a throwback to another time.

A string of sconces lit the corridor.

The rubber runner ran to the end.

At the end of the corridor, Zene threw a switch to turn off lights, leaving the only light streaming through the glass door of Alfred's office.

Zene waited outside the door. Hearing nothing, he tried the knob. Locked. With the second key, he opened the door.

The office was the old-fashioned kind. There was a reception-ist's area with a phone, a typewriter, a desk lamp. A milk glass door separated the office from the surgery. The old, thick kind. Quiet glass. History. Nothing had changed since the beginning of dental time. This was a space every dentist, any dentist knew.

In the waiting room, four chrome and old and not-well-kept-up Naugahyde chairs. Large, long, leather sofa. An ashtray on a chrome stand stood now as decoration under a no-smoking sign on the wall. The sign was embroidered to look like a sampler, the kind they used to make with each letter of the alphabet in a different color and stitch.

Zene took a cleansing breath and eased the door closed. He didn't know what the sound of a dentist doing his lab work would be, but complete silence it was not.

He heard a steady, hissing noise, air escaping from a hose. A streak of light. The click of a door closing.

He heard a sound in the hallway. Footsteps past the doorway. Quick steps. The click of high heels. A woman fast-walking.

Then silence again.

He hesitated. What he had to do didn't need thought. It was best not to think. Hesitation led to thought. Thought led to philosophy and he didn't need to be philosophical about death, because there was nothing philosophical about death. It was best to walk in and kill. He had rehearsed it to the point. Kill a man, no different than beheading a chicken, gutting a snake, slaughtering a pig. Death.

And then, in his silence, and to his surprise, he knew something was driving him, sweeping up and over him, filling his mouth and his brain with something new and frightening and awful, and that something was hatred.

Planned as you would plan an exercise, the exercise was an exercise in abstraction—death. Dead.

No.

He knew he had taken the challenge, planned the killing, because he was full of hatred of a kind he had never known and he knew that with this killing he would become pure hatred and after that—nothing.

He hated Von Stebbin.

He didn't know Von Stebbin. He had never seen Von Stebbin, but he hated him. Von Stebbin was a man who should have been blissful. He had money, he had a big house, he had a beautiful wife. The world had been kind to him. Good to him. He had done nothing to deserve those gifts. He woke up every day and he had a future, a life, a past. He should have been a model, the ideal man.

But he had turned into a whining, ugly, miserable, petty man who didn't know what he had. A despicable little pool of slime dedicated to killing his wife.

He had everything.

Zene had nothing.

If Zene burned down Alfred's house, Alfred could get a new house, the insurance would handle it.

And Zene had nothing.

If he wrecked Alfred's car, the insurance would get Alfred another one.

If someone stole Alfred's car, the police would find it. And Zene had nothing.

If Alfred didn't like his wife, he was free to trade her in for a new model.

Von Stebbin had an inside track to winning.

Tonight, he was going to lose.

Zene was going to take the only thing that Von Stebbin couldn't replace.

Blackjack in hand, Zene pushed on the milk-glass door.

And there, at the threshold of death, he stopped.

He did not understand what he was looking at.

It had once been a dental lab. But now—instruments scattered, glass broken—molds of teeth decorated the floor, teeth in a graveyard.

One of the things on the floor was the body of a man.

Alfred.

Sitting, Alfred leaned against a wall, a man stretched out to take a nap, his head bent to one side, his chin resting on his chest. Glasses askew, raised over one eyebrow. Mouth open, a frothy death-cream spilled over the blood splashed on his shirt. A lamp, tossed, cut a shadow over the body darkening the legs and feet, highlighting the torso and head.

Zene sniffed the air—the smell of blood and excrement. He knew the smell of death. The smell of death was always blood and shit. His first impulse was to leave, close the door. Leave.

But he went to the body. He knelt. Von Stebbin had been dead for minutes. Half an hour before, Karizma had called to make sure he was there and now he was dead.

Throat slashed.

A flash, a reflection, a bright reflection in a corner a few feet from the corpse. A scalpel. Bright and lethal. Smeared fingerprints. A flower of blood glistened on the wall. Someone had hurled the scalpel against the wall, slashed Von Stebbin's throat, then hurled the scalpel away.

While Zene had waited for Karizma to call, someone had killed Alfred.

Zene had seen no one leave the building.

He had heard footsteps. High-heeled footsteps.

Minutes ahead of the police? Doomed.

He pocketed the blackjack.

Karizma had taken care of Alfred.

Hard Right Turn

He walked to the car, his mind at rest.

He sat thinking for a time about impossible contingencies.

And then, he laughed. A macabre, near-silent snigger.

Whoever killed Alfred had done Zene a favor.

He drove over Greenwood up to Holman Road, stopped at a phone booth on the corner.

He dialed.

She didn't answer.

He hung up.

Back in the car.

A glance at his watch.

He drove to Aurora.

Zene felt a creeping jubilation.

He turned left onto 85th Street and as he waited for the light at Wallingford, he felt buoyant, giddy. Alfred was dead and he hadn't killed him.

He felt good.

For the first time in years, he felt good. He merged into traffic on I-5 and rolled down the window and dropped the key he had used to open the office door onto the concrete. Across the Ship Canal Bridge, he took the Roanoke Street exit. He waited for the light at Harvard and Roanoke.

He left the car at the park. He still wore the gloves. He walked the block back to the house. It was dark.

He hesitated, stopped, trying to remember why he was there. All he had to do was walk away, wait until things settled down.

Then they could be together. But he needed to see her, right then.

He stood on the sidewalk, looking up, searching for a light.

Darkness made him uneasy.

The front door was open. A strip of black nothing between the door edge and the jamb. It made no sense.

Only then did he feel a stab of panic. He knew.

No breath, just the thump in his heart. His footsteps on the brick loud as gunshots. He knew she was dead. He pushed the door open.

He waited in the heavy silence, grey light filtering through from outside, filing away the sharp edges of familiar objects— vases, greyish lumps in a somber, wooden field, lamps stood as shadows against walls, silent sentries, the furniture poised on the brink of forever silence. He knew.

In the kitchen, he heard the refrigerator kick on. He started upstairs. He took the first cautious step, the wood creaked with each step. He knew.

He stopped on the landing. A sliver of light beamed from under the door to her room. He knew.

The door opened.

Karizma stood in the doorway. She wore a brilliant white nightgown. Her skin shimmered that unique sheen—neither black nor white—her eyes still the same cat coal-like eyes that glowed in the dark. He knew.

No smile on the lips, only a smear of cruel red that made Zene breathe slow and deep. He knew.

Hovering beside her, the woman with fuchsia hair spread over her shoulders, the light from behind her turned it into an angelic, purplish nimbus framing her face.

There was a darkness in her hand, an evil darkness that shouldn't be there.

Didn't have to be there. Zene knew he was dead.

Karizma.

He watched her eyes, the glistening eyes, narrow.

She pulled him into her gaze.

Suspended him in desire—a river of memory connecting them.

Her mouth opened, the raw vestige of a kiss on her lips.

She pulled the trigger of the darkness built into her hand, a darkness he had seen before, darkness that had been there from the beginning of time. Zene knew.

The burning in him. The tearing of him. The anguish of it—another rejection added to his memory of holes he had fallen into, was falling into. Falling.

The second slug hurled him against and over the banister and took him around the horn and he flipped out into space and the falling was another fall, nothing that hadn't happened to him before, and he sprawled on the living room floor, on his back, face up, ashamed, guilty, ground down, worn out.

He didn't ask why. He knew why. It was what he expected—the one, the only one sure thing that erased him.

And in his blood, he saw the end of hope. Hope an illusion that had kept him alive long enough to see her again and once having seen her, it was enough.

Tetelestai.

He looked up and into the leering maw of infinity seeing her leaning over the banister, still holding the pistol, her hair still that angelic halo. He raised a hand, a signal, calling her, but she did not smile. He whispered thank you and his hand dropped to his heart and he sank

Zene walking down Eastlake, the shoulders of his parka stuffed with money, fifty-dollar bills, enough money for the ticket for the crossing. No beer. No wine.

Just the crossing now.

His heels crackle on the sidewalk, horrendous thunder in the everlasting silence spiced with the screech of vehicles with flashing lights streaming along Eastlake, hearses smothered in the grey shadows of undertakers and to his left, the noise of I-5—the buzz and hum of cars with people going places—and to his right, Lake Union rimmed with houseboats, dead in the night, no lights on the lake, and to his deep right, the George Washington Memorial Bridge on the Lincoln Highway lit with suicide-lights, a string of yellow lights, light yellow ribbons in a young girl's hair, but no life in them now, in the suicide hour, 3:00 a.m., and he reaches the fork where Eastlake fades into Fairview, and he passes the Eastlake power station lit up with blinking red flares on the now dead smokestacks that no longer spew the residue of light into the dark and he walks on through the moaning center of a dying city, down, down, down dead to King Street, to the King Street Station and down the stairs, down more, down past the red lights of the cop cruiser and into the building built so long ago, long ago, and standing looking up at the schedule board, he checks departure times, leave times—the train to Vancouver four-thirty, dead-head—and he lies down on the bench, the lights, fading, old, greying lights that had shone too long in a too dark place, and he takes a deep breath, his mind fading, hands folded over his parka stuffed with fifty dollar bills. The voice on the sound system announces the Vancouver train.

Zene stands. Heavy now growing lighter.

He walks out of the station onto the platform.

He walks to the edge of the platform.

At the edge of the platform, he steps off.

Facing him, the tunnel under the city.

He walks north between the twin rails, north.

Ahead of him, the mouth of the tunnel, the tunnel under the city.

The tunnel under the city is dark.

Zene walks into darkness.

Into silence.

About the Author

Drawing by Larry Crist.

Jack Remick is a novelist, poet, essayist. His work includes the novels—*Blood; Gabriela and The Widow; Citadel; Doubles in a Game of Chance*. The poetry—*Satori, Poems*. The essays—*What Do I Know*.

Other works by Jack Remick

Gabriela and The Widow, Coffeetown Press.

Blood, Coffeetown Press.

Citadel, Quartet Global.

Josie Delgado, A Poem of the Central Valley, Quartet Global

No Century for Apologies, Quartet Global

Pieces, Quartet Global.

The Deification, Coffeetown Press.

Valley Boy, Coffeetown Press.

The Book of Changes, Coffeetown Press.

Throwback and Other Stories, Quartet Global.

Trio of Lost Souls, Coffeetown Press.

The Weekend Novelist Writes a Mystery
(Co-author with Robert J. Ray), Dell Trade Paper.

Doubles in a Game of Chance—The Sixth Sense, Quartet Global.

What Do I Know? Essays, Sidekick Press

S.B. VPMR, Quartet Global

Terminal Weird, Black Heron Press.

Lemon Custard, Quartet Global.

Falcon, Quartet Global.

Satori, Poems, Coffeetown Press.

Maxine, Quartet Global.

One Year in the Time of Violence, Quartet Global.

Pacific Coast Highway, Quartet Global.

Black Madonna in Blue, Quartet Global.